Long ago, when the powers of good and evil were younger than now…

TRAVELS IN NHEARN

-PART II-

-CHOICE-

A STORY IN THE WORLD CREATED BY

Jared S DuBose

Dedicated to my fourth grade teacher
who compromised with my writing lessons and let
me explore my imagination

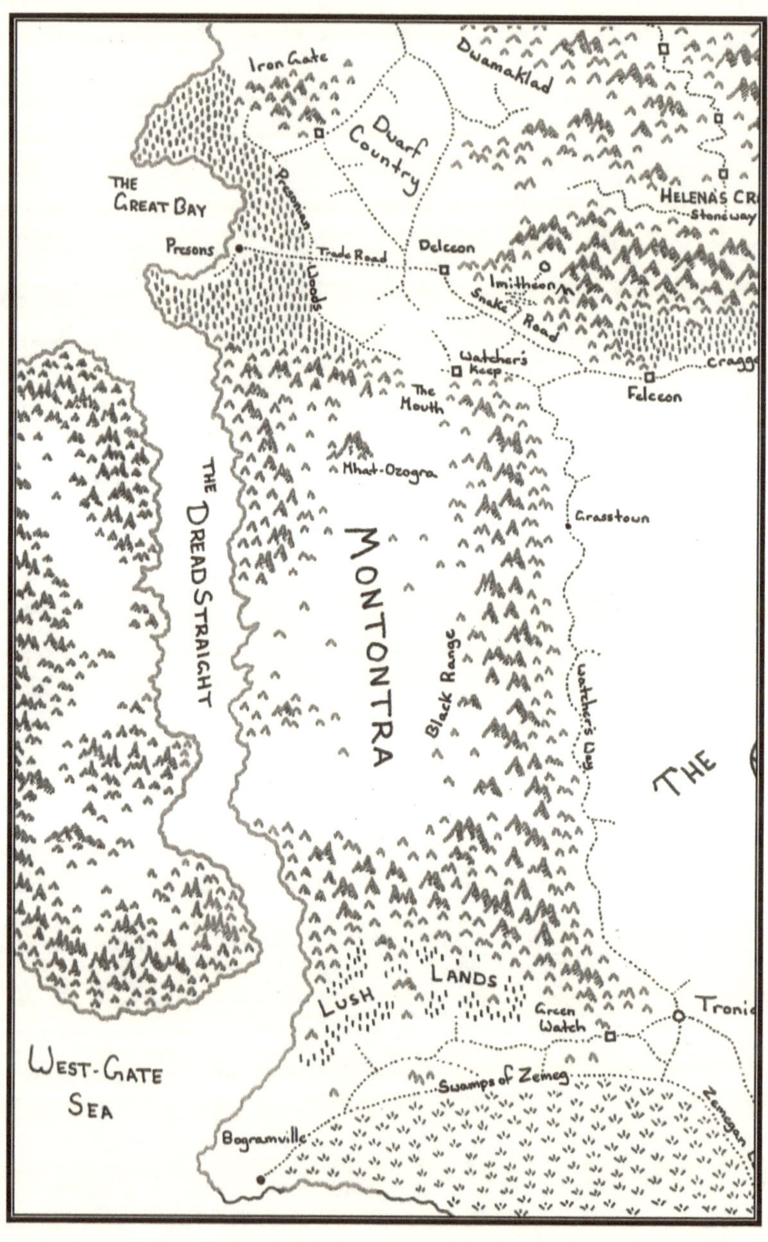

Iron Gate
Dwamaklad
Duarf Country
THE GREAT BAY
HELENAS CR
Stoneway
Presons
Precorous Woods
Trade Road
Delceon
Imitheon
Snake Road
Watcher's Keep
The Mouth
Felceon
Cragg
Mhat-Ozogra
Grasstown
MONTONTRA
Black Range
Watcher's Way
THE DREAD STRAIGHT
THE
LUSH LANDS
Green Watch
Tronic
West-Gate Sea
Swamps of Zemeg
Bogramville
Nemegan

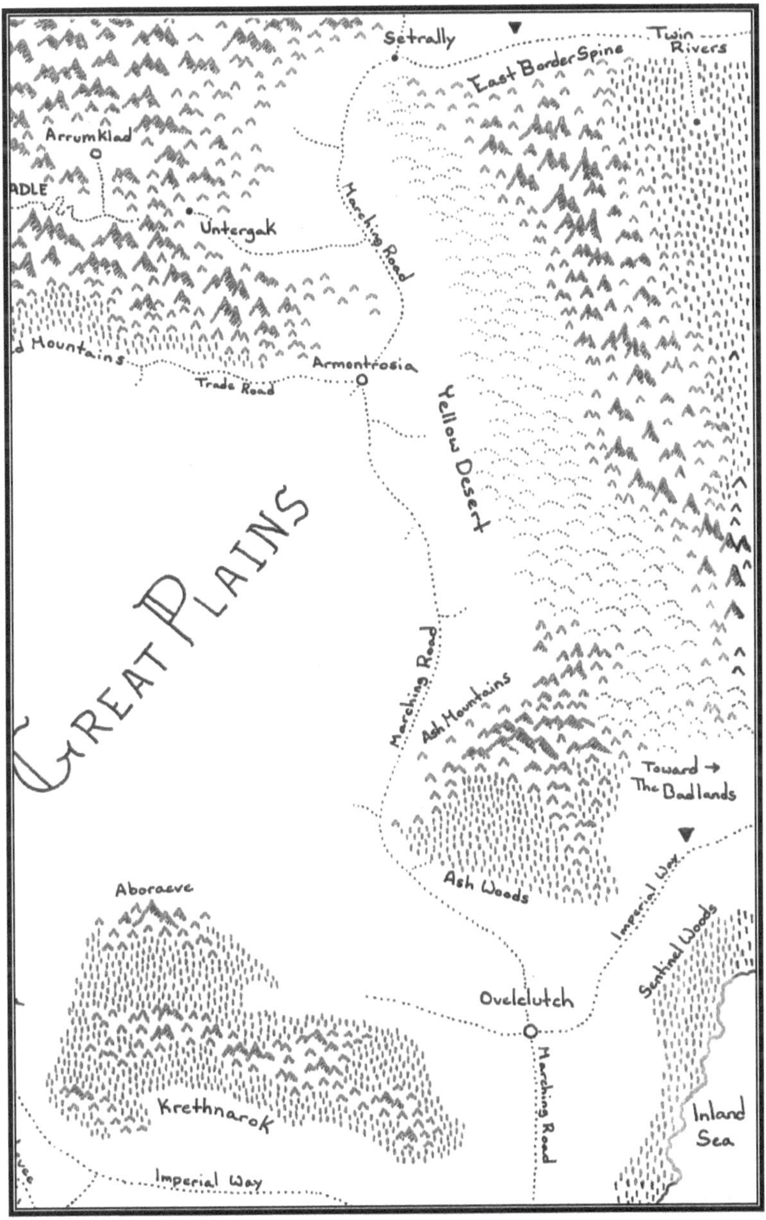

Setrally
East Border Spine
Twin Rivers
Arrumklad
ADLE
Untergak
Marching Road
d Mountains
Trade Road
Armontrosia
Yellow Desert
GREAT PLAINS
Marching Road
Ash Mountains
Toward →
The Badlands
Ash Woods
Imperial Way
Aboraeve
Sentinel Woods
Ovelclutch
Krethnarok
Marching Road
Imperial Way
Inland Sea

-CONTENTS-

PROLOGUE:
THE COMING
OF THE HIGHBORNE

Ænoen and the gods who loved Nhearn kept a close and silent watch over their world, waiting for a day that Annabel's wickedness might reveal itself once again. For many eons nothing had yet been witnessed and the gods became complacent. With long years stretching into ages after the creation, with nothing new developed by their divine hands, Ænoen called upon the Heavens and brought forth Christianna to share her grace upon Nhearn.

"Daughter of Gold, Keeper of Heaven, I have waited long ages and trust now that goodness may be done once more. Upon this place we all have made, I would wish for noise. Silence has sat for too long in our home, and it is time we create newness once more."

"I will grace the world we have made, for not a gift, nor a hand, have I yet offered to our common home. I will bring them from my realm above, virtuous and curious creatures besides ourselves who we might speak with and guide forth." Christianna raised her hands and the golden gates of her realm opened wide. "I cannot craft, nor can I create, for it was not my purpose to do so. Instead I have rescued what came from the dark and what has seen my light. I have chosen seven that Istalebreth before us had sewn."

"They are invited," Ænoen proclaimed. "They will come and exist upon this place that we have made together."

From the golden gates of Heaven they arrived, seven identical creatures whose stature was lesser than gods but greater than what was to come after. Upon a great mountain, where the peak had been made into a wide flat stage before the threshold of Heaven, they stepped upon Nhearn beneath the midday light of Ænoen's Sol.

"Welcome, Highborne," Ænoen so named the seven. "Come and find joy within our common home. It has been made by all the hands of those before your coming and is meant to be loved for as long as you shall exist upon it."

The Highborne were filled with an abundance of joy, for below the mountain summit, to the very horizon of the world, were sights so grand it made them weep with delight.

"Christianna, Keeper of Heaven, Daughter of Gold, and Watcher of the Day, has invited you, and I welcome you." Ænoen walked beside them as they neared the edge of the mountain flat. "I wish for you all to find joy and love within all that you see. Choose and make for yourselves homes across this place we all have made. Fill it with wondrous noise and hymn so that we before you may also find joy." With a smile and hope in his heart that the silence of Nhearn could be broken, Ænoen sent the seven Highborne free into the lands beyond.

As the Highborne began their descent from the mountain along a staircase that was carved with purpose across the spine of the rise, the watchful eyes of the full moon rose over the horizon. Silver light covered them all but the Highborne were not distracted away from the great world before them, all save one.

The lone Highborne gazed into the moonlight, but it never shied away or resisted its power. Aurora, Guardian of Nhearn, Daughter of Silver, left her noble post upon the moon and arrived upon the stair to study down upon the Highborne. All of the others continued on their journey and left behind the first Highborne so that they may speak alone with the Goddess.

"Who are you," Aurora asked. "Speak to me."

And the Highborne spoke then, "I am a Highborne, rescued from the gloom of the Abyss by a halo of gold, and I have been invited here by the Lord Ænoen."

"Why is it that you would wish to witness me?"

And the Highborne answered then, "I felt your silver light and I see the moon as it has seen me. I have not seen before such grace, nor have I felt such goodness."

Aurora was enamored and she climbed the mountain to meet with Christianna at the golden gates of Heaven. "Keeper of the Heavens, Daughter of Gold, I have met with one of your seven. I ask that they may come to me so that I might teach them of my ways. With my knowledge and purpose, I would lend to the Highborne all that I may."

"Watcher of the Moon, Daughter of Silver, with love, you may teach the Highborne of your ways."

Aurora returned to the Highborne and showed him righteousness. He was taught to judge others for their deeds. He was shown what evil was and how to remove such things from the world. Aurora then gave to the Highborne a silver sword, a sliver of the moon itself, and he was given purpose. "Keep watch and all of Nhearn shall be safe. Remain good and I shall honor you always."

With her departure the Highborne returned to the other Highborne who had continued the descent without him. As the seven adventured away from Ænoen's high place near Christianna's Heaven, they found a wild and untamed woodland. Within were dark shadows as the canopy above absorbed the light of Sol. Trees, vines, grasses, and shrubs grew all about, disarrayed and natural across the landscape.

Six of the Highborne chose to go around, wandering the forest border to continue their discoveries of Nhearn, yet one alone entered the woods. Within this place he found abundant life and exotic wonder. He did not find horror, nor darkness, but shade and comfort. The vast woodlands were explored and happiness was found within this place. Upon the highest branches of the greatest tree, Vanessa revealed herself upon Nhearn and came to the Highborne.

"Who are you," Vanessa asked. "Speak to me."

And the Highborne spoke then, "I am a Highborne, rescued from the gloom of the Abyss by a halo of gold, and I have been invited here by the Lord Ænoen."

"Why is it that you would wish to witness me?"

And the Highborne answered then, "I felt your beauty and I see the woodlands. I have not seen before such wonder, nor have I felt such gladness."

Vanessa was joyed and she climbed the mountain to meet with Christianna at the golden gates of Heaven. "Keeper of the Heavens, Daughter of Gold, I have met with one of your seven. I ask that they may come to me so that I might teach them of my ways. With my knowledge and purpose, I would lend to the Highborne all that I may."

"Creator of the Woodlands, Daughter of Change, with love, you may teach the Highborne of your ways."

Vanessa went to the Highborne and showed him the woodlands of her creation. He was taught to enjoy the trees and live from the fruit. He was shown what change was and how to overcome through uncertainty. He was given all of Vannessa's works to live in. "Tend to these places and all of Nhearn shall be wondrous. Enjoy always and I shall honor you." The Highborne remained within that place with Vanessa and changed with the seasons as she so desired.

Six Highborne continued their journey and they explored more of Nhearn. As they traveled further they discovered their paths blocked by a rise of such height that only the stone showed bare above them. Five of the Highborne chose to go around, wandering the lower foothills to continue their discoveries of Nhearn, yet one alone climbed up. Within this place he found bountiful riches and incredible wonder. He did not find desolation, nor difficulty, but surety and dwelling. The grand mountains were explored and happiness was found within this place. Upon the highest peaks of the greatest mountain, Helena revealed herself upon Nhearn and came to the Highborne.

"Who are you," Helena asked. "Speak to me."

And the Highborne spoke then, "I am a Highborne, rescued from the gloom of the Abyss by a halo of gold, and I have been invited here by the Lord Ænoen."

"Why is it that you would wish to witness me?"

And the Highborne answered then, "I felt your splendor and I see the mountains. I have not seen before such wonder, nor have I felt such gladness."

Helena was softened and she climbed the mountain to meet with Christianna at the golden gates of Heaven. "Keeper of the Heavens, Daughter of Gold, I have met with one of your seven. I ask that they may come to me so that I might teach them of my ways. With my knowledge and purpose, I would lend the Highborne all that I may."

"Crafter of the Mountains, Daughter of the Earth, with love, you may teach the Highborne of your ways."

Helena went to the Highborne and showed him the mountains of her creation. He was taught to respect the stone and live from the mineral. He was shown what constancy was and how to weather through uncertainty. He was given all of Helena's works to live in. "Craft in these places and all of Nhearn shall be wondrous. Honor it always and I shall honor you." The Highborne remained within that place with Helena and resisted the passing of time as she so desired.

Five Highborne continued their journey and they explored more of Nhearn. As they did the dwindling number found their path was denied to them by a thundering river. Four of the Highborne chose to find another pass, seeking shallower shores to calm fords, yet one alone dove in. Within this place he found limitless power and sublime pleasure. He did not find despair, nor ruin, but confidence and relaxation. The river was explored and happiness was found within this place. Within the roughest rapids of the grandest river, Anastasia revealed herself upon Nhearn and came to the Highborne.

"Who are you," Anastasia asked. "Speak to me."

And the Highborne spoke then, "I am a Highborne, rescued from the gloom of the Abyss by a halo of gold, and I have been invited here by the Lord Ænoen."

"Why is it that you would wish to witness me?"

And the Highborne answered then, "I felt your power and I see the waters. I have not seen before such wonder, nor have I felt such gladness."

Anastasia was overcome and she climbed the mountain to meet with Christianna at the golden gates of Heaven. "Keeper of the Heavens, Daughter of Gold, I have met with one of your seven. I ask that they may come to me so that I might teach them of my ways. With my knowledge and purpose I would lend to the Highborne all that I may."

"Carver of the Rivers, Daughter of Water, with love, you may teach the Highborne of your ways."

Anastasia went to the Highborne and showed him the seas of her creation. He was taught to brave the currents and live from the bounty of the waters. He was shown what rhythm was and how to react with uncertainty. He was given all of Anastasia's works to live in. "Swim in these places and all of Nhearn shall be wondrous. Drift always and I shall honor you." The Highborne remained within that place with Anastasia and fluxed with the tides as she so desired.

Four Highborne continued their journey and they explored more of Nhearn. As they did the smaller group found that their path was ravaged by a vicious storm. Three of the Highborne chose to find another route, traveling in the clear skies under Sol, yet one alone pushed through. Within this place he found tremendous energy and deafening noise. He did not find destruction, nor resistance, but refreshment and song. The clouds were explored and happiness was found within this place. Within the strongest gusts of the darkest cloud, Katrina revealed herself upon Nhearn and came to the Highborne.

"Who are you," Katrina asked. "Speak to me."

And the Highborne spoke then, "I am a Highborne, rescued from the gloom of the Abyss by a halo of gold, and I have been invited here by the Lord Ænoen."

"Why is it that you would wish to witness me?"

And the Highborne answered then, "I felt your music and I see the skies. I have not seen before such wonder, nor have I felt such gladness."

Katrina was serendipitous and she climbed the mountain to meet with Christianna at the golden gates of Heaven. "Keeper of the Heavens, Daughter of Gold, I have met with one of your seven. I ask that they may come to me so that I might teach them of my ways. With my knowledge and purpose I would lend to the Highborne all that I may."

"Conjurer of the Clouds, Daughter of the Air, with love you may teach the Highborne of your ways."

Katrina went to the Highborne and showed him the sky of her creation. He was taught to use the winds and live from the harvests. He was shown what pleasantness was and how to avoid uncertainty. He was given all of Katrina' works to live in. "Sing in these places and all of Nhearn shall be wondrous. Grow always and I shall honor you." The Highborne remained within that place with Katrina and shifted on the winds as she so desired.

Three Highborne continued their journey and they explored more of Nhearn. As they did, the trio found that their path had led to a land beyond the edge of safety. Only one of the Highborne stood confidently, glowing with the radiance of the moon, and he carried a vibrant sword, though he never led the others. He remained a full pace behind the Highborne and watched the other two closely. Together they continued and the edge of Nhearn neared them.

In a realm away from all wonder they had come, and within they did not find any pleasure, nor did they discover any comfort, but they knew fear then. Above them was a dark orb, the corrupted moon, rising from the edge of the world, and all around was a shroud that hid all the joy of Nhearn away from them.

"Who are you," the darkness hissed. "Speak to me now!"

And the Highborne said nothing.

From within the shroud of darkness, from a deep pit of pure despair, from where wonders were unable to be revealed, arrived a Goddess who was eclipsed entirely by the dark orb above and she remained hidden from the light of Sol. The earth was sundered beneath her, the waters were parched from about her, the air was stale around her, and nothing dared to grow within her sight. "Why is it that you wish now that you had not witnessed me?"

Only one of the Highborne answered the Goddess then, "Do not cast me away! I can feel your power and I have earned your worth. I have not ever before seen such terror nor felt such awe. Accept me, as the others who have been chosen before me! Accept me!"

The radiant Highborne stood and watched as the final two companions were set before what he knew to be the great evil that Aurora had warned of. The Highborne who demanded the affection of the wicked one continued, "This other Highborne has come this far only with the help of all the others. He has earned nothing himself, and he has no worth such as I. This one relied on the woodlands for its fruits, and the mountains for its riches, and the waters for their bounty, and the air for its harvests, and even the moon for its protection. I have earned all this way with effort of my own making, for not a thing have I taken or borrowed to come here, to at last stand before you at the ends of the world. Cast out this one, take I who has been made stronger. Take me who must be chosen, and then leave this other to their fate."

And the vile darkness answered the Highborne, "You will come with me willingly, and you will be as devout in purpose as you are pathetic in plight. I will not allow you to become as the others, but instead you will be to me exactly what it is you offer yourself as: an instrument."

The Highborne was not asked for at the golden gates of Heaven as the others had been, and the darkness did not climb the summits of the distant mountain to request from Christianna her devotion or to state their purpose before accepting them. Annabel, under the darkness of the corrupted moon at the edge of the world all the other gods had created, took the Highborne into her dominion and showed him all the terrors that she could manifest before the creation of Istalebreth broke in her hands as she so desired.

CHAPTER I
THE GREAT PLAINS

Basimick wandered into the grasslands and found that he had no direction except *away*. Ovelclutch was kept at his back, the smoke plume directing him as the city fell below the horizon and out of view. He went at a quick pace to try and escape the noise of violence which seemed to chase him as the agony of the attack grew fiercer still. As the sound that carried on the wind dwindled to silence at last, his pace across the empty lands fell. The smoke still showed plainly no matter his distance, like an evil sentinel in the sky, and as night began to arrive there was a foul glow that kept the cloud visible in the dark. He continued away from it, using the fire as his only guide, for there was nothing else in the great empty distance ahead.

Morning came, he had walked the whole night without rest, and through the day he continued until night was falling again. Still the glow haunted him, and it seemed fiercer than the previous night. As Basimick neared the rise of one of the many hills, he turned toward the plume and braved to look at it, but as he glanced at the glow he shied away so that his gaze went quickly toward the ground. He pulled out the hunter's tokens from the pocket in his jerkin and rolled each of them in his fingers. He remained silent in the darkness, for there were no words he could share with the night that could make him feel better for leaving his companions in the city. *Go get help, you lived for a reason.*

Basimick took a few deep breaths before returning to his journey. As he wandered deeper into the grasslands the wind began to rustle in the grasses, and as another dawn came, the sky revealed a gloomy morning. The smoke had settled, the plume became a stinking smog, and ash fell under a hazy red sun. The quiet of the landscape began to bother him, for it offered no distractions from himself.

The elves attacked the dwarves, killed them all. His mind was quick and his hand clutched to the pommel of his sword as the intrusive thoughts came to him. *They must have killed all of the others too.* He let go of the sword and felt for the coins in his pocket, but as he did he could feel the ridges of the printed scales across his leather jerkin. His hand fell back to his sword as he walked onward. *Why did we have to be there when it happened?*

Basimick woke and it was night again. He could not recall falling asleep, but when he had risen he was more stiff and weak than before. He could no longer see a glow of fire, but the smoke had stolen the stars from the sky and there was nothing except the stark darkness. All around him was a whispering breeze through the grasses, though nothing else made noise.

It was dark, difficult to orient, and Basimick became aware of his predicament. He tried to move, feeling for the heights of grasses around him with his fingers and treading carefully to avoid pits in the ground with purposeful steps forward. He eventually came to a steep rise and crawled slowly to the mount, but the night was inescapable. The plains did not reveal any light, show any signs, nor was there a distance that allowed any clear sky to prevail. His eyes grew pained as they widened in the absolute darkness and he had to shut them tightly to recover. Blind in the dark, Basimick stood as still as he could. From the base of the hill he could hear the wind thrashing in the grass. It swept from behind him and encircled the hill before the gust rushed away into the silent night as though it had fled.

Dawn passed without Basimick and the day was cast in an orange hue due to the heavy cloud of smoke. The yellow grasses that appeared endless now blended at the horizon so that his tired eyes could not differentiate the earth from the sky. Before him was an endless landscape without landmarks, without paths, and without others to lead the way. Thoughts of loneliness were quickly replaced with a churning noise uttered from the depths of his stomach.

He had not thought of food, for fear had been fueling him, but after several days, some he couldn't recollect for exhaustion, it became a forefront need. There were no trees, no bulbs in the ground either, nor were there birds or creatures that he had seen to attempt to capture. Basimick grabbed a tall shaft of grass but quickly lost interest, for chewing on nothing would be better than dry straw. His stomach made a deep angry noise but there was nothing to be done for it.

Basimick looked one last time around all horizons as he stood on a hilltop above the plains, but there wasn't anything to see. Hopeful that food or water was out there to be found, he began walking once more. "No point in staying here," he said aloud to himself, but his voice scared him in the lonely place, and he walked silently throughout the rest of the day.

Unknown spans had passed beneath him and he tried once again to see any landmark or signs of life by gaining height over the grasses. He struggled to make it to the top of a large hill, but disappointment quickly befell him as nothing revealed itself from the vantage. A breeze picked up and swept over the hill suddenly, rustling the grasses as it arrived. Without any direction he decided to put the wind at his back and he marched on. As the thoughts of Kurrum began to arrive and the grip to the hilt of the sword grew tense, the wind stopped blowing.

"Who," the wind suddenly rushed over his ears with a whisper carried upon it. As though the plains were breathing in and out, the gust suddenly changed direction to push against his chest. "Fah," the wind rushed over him again and nearly pushed him down.

He let go of the sword and turned away from the dust that was being swelled up in the ravaging winds. Beneath the cover of his hands he looked skyward. Basimick could not hope for direction from the breeze and he tried his best to guess where the sun was for the time of day, though he knew not the hour. He attempted northward and westward to his best judgment, and he walked into an endless grassland where he could see into the distance that the wind was rolling like waves across the plain.

Night was falling and Basimick had to adjust his course several times as delirium misguided him. "Who," the wind rushed through the grass. "Fah," the gusts rippled on the grass back toward him. His stomach growled with the howling wind. There was still no sign of food, no offering of a trail, and still no life to be seen. *Go get help, you lived for a reason,* but the thought was becoming more and more disparaging instead of helpful.

Dusk came and as the vibrant red glare of sunset ended Basimick heard a charging soldier behind him. He turned and a powerful gust of wind knocked him over onto his back. "Who," the gale called to him as he raced to stand back up. "Fah," the wind seemed to say as it passed and the grass against a nearby hillside shook as the howling zephyr crashed into it. In the waning light he could see the air move across the hillside and back into the dales. Basimick hoped that the open air atop the hill might be a sanctuary from the aggressive wind rushing between the hills and he began to run up to its height.

Dark came fast, but even the departure of day did not save him from the vicious gale. Throughout the night he could feel the terrible winds rushing around the hill, swirling around him as though it were studying him, and in the dark of night, sleep eventually captured him.

East to west, rise then fall, day then night, Basimick continued to wander northward as best he could by guessing direction from the sun which could now be made out in a heavy glare against the smoke that had begun to clear, but the vast emptiness of the grasslands made any sense of direction difficult. Using only the silhouettes of hills on the horizon or the heights of grasses as landmarks for guidance, he would adjust his trek toward north into the plains. He kept moving, but the grass, like hypnotic waves in the breeze, were disorienting, and the open sun that had once been hiding in the smoke began to make the long journey painful. His skin began to rash under the heat of the sun and his mouth became parched.

It was twilight on what he believed to be the fifth, or perhaps the seventh day, when Basimick found a dry creek bed between two sizable hills. The bottom of the dusty dale was calm with exception to brief and sudden gusts of haunting winds through the ravine of the dead river banks and the hills that hid the old place from the rest of the plains. *Better than wind all the time*, he thought as he looked up at the grasses swaying about atop the hills around him in the waning light.

Basimick undid the buckle of his sheath and lowered his empty pack along with his sword into the dust of the dead riverbed. He looked toward where he thought Ovelclutch should be, but there wasn't a glow of fire like the first night, or even the dark smoke plume to cover the stars and steal what little bit of light that the night had to offer him. It was clear and moonless so that all about were soft twinkles of silver starlight.

As he prepared to rest for the night, a strong gale rushed through the crevice of the river banks. It forced the dust of the ancient creek into the air and it surrounded him so that the silhouettes of the hills in the night were no longer beside him. "Who," the gust shouted at him and then it swelled back the opposite way as though it were attempting to devour him. "Fah," it repeated as the wind drew into the lungs of the world. Basimick grabbed his pack and sword before the air stole them away.

With an arm to cover his face he crept out of the dust funnel and made his way to the height of the hill nearby, hoping that the top might offer him sanctuary again. He looked around and in the twinkling of starlight he could see the grass part ways like a beast were rushing up the hillside to chase him. It was a wild thing that leapt from the grasses toward him and it flew over the hill upon the wind. It was a creature with a back full of porcelain quills, its belly was the color of blood, and its face was that of a gigantic skull come back to life. "Who," it howled as it passed him. "Fah," it shrieked as it landed beneath the summit and turned to rush back up across the opposite side of the hill.

The monster was then holding a great white stick in its hands and they spun the weapon so that the grasses were whipped in a gale summoned by the monster's own skill. "Hoopha! Hoopha, Hoopha, Hoopha!" The skull creature chanted in many different voices that were carried away from it upon the swift wind as it began a wild charge with an unnatural speed. Basimick was certain that the wild terror would trample over the top of him, but as it came within distance to strike, a powerful wind erupted from the creature and overcame him. With a heavy blast he was thrown to the ground. Dust spun around in a twisting tendril to show that the wind had once again changed direction, a whistling noise guiding the gusts, and in the air was the haunt before it lowered to the ground and divided the grasses in a breeze that seemed to be surrounding the being.

Basimick got to his knees and grabbed up the scabbard that had left his grasp. "Hoopha," he could hear another gale growing in the grasses, the shout of the terrible creature gaining speed toward his hilltop. He turned to greet it and with fear in his heart he pulled out his father's sword from its sheath, but the wind roared before shoving him to the ground. Basimick looked up at the wild creature, regained his wits, and lunged for the sword that had been flung away from him. On his back, Basimick pointed the sword at the horror with the thought to strike.

"Stay back," he yelled. "Whatever you are, stay back from me!"

"Hoopha," the monster twirled the spear in its hands over its head and began to hover over the hilltop. A churning of dust and loose grass swirled into a tornado that pushed the wild creature higher than Basimick could reach.

As the monster prepared to lunge from the height, Basimick stood up and pointed the sword at it, both hands gripping the hilt to brace for the charge. Suddenly, on the horizon, the silver light of the moon lit the hilltop as it rose into the dark night. The land became clear, hills cast long shadows over the plains, and the grass became splendid in the magical light.

Basimick looked again at the monster and the tip of his sword lowered away from a violent pose. The skull was that of a large fanged cat, but the depths of the sockets glared in the moonlight with eyes more like his own. The spear had a shining metal tip and was held in hands that did not take the form of a dangerous creature. The porcelain quills were pulled through a cloak that fluttered in the wind and the red belly of the beast was not unlike the dragon scaled jerkin that he wore himself.

The sword was set upon the ground and he raised his hands toward the creature in the night sky. "Who are you?"

It did not answer, but the gale began to vanish and the loose debris that had been caught in the funnel began to fall across the hillside away from Basimick. The being started to lower to the hilltop and the spear tip was pointed upward to avoid a threatening presence.

Basimick kept his hands raised, "Am I a threat to you?"

"Common speak," it tried to point at him, but the being's pale finger ended abruptly at the knuckle. "Dih fer'eh el Empire?"

"I don't understand," Basimick answered cautiously, hoping that the being would understand him. "Do you speak common?"

"Some," it said coldly.

"Have you been the one following me?"

"You have trespassed in my lands, Imperial."

"I didn't mean to. I am lost out here. Will you help me find the way out so that I am not trespassing? I mean no harm to you."

The being was silent for a moment and it began to lift away from the ground as a gentle breeze swelled beneath its feet. "You come armed," it pointed at Basimick's sword.

Basimick lifted the scabbard to show the being his intention and he gently reclaimed the sword to put it away. "I will not use it."

"You will not harm me," it said with some confusion.

"No," and he slid the blade back into its sheath.

The being peered over the blade as it returned to its place of safety. As soon as the sword was tucked away the being began to laugh with a wild howl. They then spun the spear in their hand and became overjoyed, exclaiming, "Do se'lah dih'n pogesh!"

Basimick smiled, but he was confused. "Will you help me?"

"I see now that you have a bigger role to play," the being hovered into the sky before striking the ground with its white staff. The being pulled itself back to the earth against the wind that seemed to tug on them toward the sky. "They came for myself," it said to

Basimick as it neared him. "The old spirits. I was once made a great monster in my prime, but now I am able to see as they do with many long years," the being pointed to the sky with a wounded finger and it pulled on the staff to get close enough to whisper with Basimick.

The skull did not move as it spoke, but the gleam of the being's eyes twinkled in the moonlight from the depths of the black sockets. "I must protect the land from what may happen. Without myself, the grasslands will end. It was protected by the lush, but now all is doomed to wither." The being spun around the staff gently, as though a dance were occurring, but the soft noise of a gentle breeze seemed to still pull upon the being. "I defend us from the lands of fire where Morganna echoes." The creature grabbed tightly to the anchored spear and held itself down so that it could stand upright upon the hilltop.

As though deep in thought, the being looked away from Basimick and stared out into the west. "E're is a fire in those lands and it burns toward the east from that place in the west. From the east the air may sweep o'r the grass e'n strike those dark mountains bare so that e're is no beauty, but it is done to remember that she is in wait. I keep those lines of glow at bay. Without me the fire yet grows."

Basimick looked at the being who wore the bones of a monster and he saw beneath the wardrobe that upon its deathly pale skin were scars of lashings that were ancient injuries more severe than any he had ever seen before. While the being looked over their lands, Basimick gently stated, "I will not hurt you."

"This is good fortune."

"Is there somewhere to go?"

"I will take you e're with haste," the being nodded and as it turned to face him. Basimick could see the glare of teeth behind a smile. "Without myself to guide, you may yet perish. Where I was able once, I see has been undone by the deeds against the lush. It was our siblings, long ago, that took to the Lady of the Wood, yet to us she was graced always by the heavens e'n swept by Katrina. In the grasses of this land we saw that it was she that was most beautiful."

Basimick was confused as the being continued telling a long tale and at times it would whisper in words that he could not comprehend. The grass around him was whipped in a violent thrashing, but he himself was in a calm center as the tornado rose to surround them both. The monster began to sing in a somber voice that carried on the breeze:

"E're do om e'aht ganna thorbranni.
There I am where the fire glows.
E'n e're el mun ec thorbranni.
And there the moon is bright.
E're do el ne're sha thorbranni.
There I am near to her shining.
E'n e're el fol ec thorbranni
And there the fall is light."

As the sad words swept away with the wind, Basimick could feel the world slip away with the breeze. He tried to understand the changing tones of the breeze as the word thorbranni repeated itself over and over, but he was pushed into a slumber, a comfort he had missed since his village, and the night overcame him.

CHAPTER II
HISSILANDA ARRIVES

The White Queen of Krethnarok entered from the western gate atop a large white stag, and walking beside her were four members of her personal guard, each of them fully adorned in silver armor so that their identities were lost in the regalia of their position. They held her white banners aloft as they came into the city and the armies of the Sentinel Woods lowered their own dark flags to respect the queen's coming. The warriors that had come from the groves of the Twin Rivers kneeled to her entourage as they moved down the main road toward the inner ring of the city and the nomads of the plains bowed with their arms across their chest as the white light of her radiance was cast upon them.

The elves that had taken Ovelclutch then banded together to work as quickly as they could to remove any signs of the incredible violence from the street so that their queen could move unimpeded toward the Iron Keep. Despite the carnage still visible throughout the avenues, the piles of dead dwarves being burned in large pyres at the crossroads, and the sounds of dwelling towers being raided for the last scrap of culture to be eradicated, Hissilanda did not move her head to witness or offer any notice of care. Even the stinking plume of smoke that lingered over the entire city did not seem to insult her senses, and she rode passed the remains of battle with a regal posture while her sight was solely fixed at the inner gate of the iron dome at the heart of the city.

Queen Hissilanda the White entered into the dazzling courtyard of the Iron Park beneath the shining dome of the Iron Keep, where Agnithia Witch-Heart herself waited with her own servants to welcome the queen to their victory. The white light of the queen passing contended with shimmering rainbows that lit the inner mall as the sun was captured by a large crystal in the center chimney of the iron dome above. Guarded by the personal servants of the elven general of the Sentinel Woods, bound and forced to kneel, was the Lord of the Iron Keep, a noble dwarf who had been discovered to be the chosen Trade Master of Ovelclutch. He had signs of being beaten and there were wounds of torture upon his limbs. His lips were split and blood crusted throughout his beard that still held most of its shape with the royal oils and waxes offered to dwarves of high stature.

Agnithia bowed only slightly and whispered through the metal mask that hid her face, "This is the last dwarf within the city, my queen. This is the trade lord of Ovelclutch."

"Damn you," the dwarf shouted in Imperial common as he prepared to stand to take action against the elven general, but the dark cloaked elven guards to either side forced him back down onto his knees as the white queen came closer. "Hell take you too, bright elf," he spat.

"You disrespect my authority, lord dwarf," Hissilanda spoke back in the human's common tongue.

She was still seated atop her white stag and her gaze fell upon the Trade Master.

"My city is in ruin and you demand my respect? My people lie dead and you are the one scorned? How dare you-"

"No need to raise your voice," she said calmly through a smirk as the echo of his shouting faded into the great heights of the courtyard. The guards gripped the dwarf's shoulders tighter so that he yipped with pain from the wounds and they shook him until he was silenced. "I will keep this brief, for I have matters of great importance to attend to elsewhere." Her tone shifted and in the dwarvish tongue she asked the Trade Master, "Where is the secret path to Arrumklad?"

"I wouldn't tell you where such a place was, even if you were King Kankor himself!"

Hissilanda looked at Agnithia and began to speak in elvish with the general, "I will need most of the allies to move northward and westward. They will move to join with Genelous and his army in Presons along with all of the military leaders of Krethnarok. We will begin a northward assault across Dwamaklad from the western side of Helena's Cradle. Sylvarath will be-"

"Dwamaklad," the Trade Master interrupted after hearing the name of the dwarven landmark through their elven dialect.

Hissilanda returned her attention to the Trade Master and began to speak in dwarven again. "You would not grace me with answers to my questions, trade lord. I will not grace you with the same."

The Trade Master bowed his head considering all that had been done to Ovelclutch. What he had assumed in witnessing the attack was that it had been motivated by the tension of building a dwarven city too close to the elven woodlands, but it dawned on him that this was not at all the end of the elves' destructive journey. "What are you doing?"

Hissilanda offered a pleasant smile, not sinister or devious, but genuine in its appearance. "I will tell you." She waved the guards off as though she were rescuing the dwarf from the coming violence. "Where is the path?"

"I don't need your answers, elf. You'll have to search for your lifetime before the way reveals itself to you. Helena keeps her secrets well." He looked at Agnithia and the dark shaeman that was always standing beside her. He erupted in the common tongue at them, "But you know that already, cultists."

"Certainly my kindness is worth the answer? I would hate to become less courteous."

"I will keep the answers to myself."

"There are ways of breaking codes and learning secrets," Hissilanda muttered, waving her hand so that the elves returned and began attacking the Trade Master with the sharp edges of their knives. The queen asked again through the dwarf's screams, "Where is the path?"

The dwarf withstood the pain for a long while. The elves cut until the sleeves of his royal uniform became ribbons, they took the jewels of his office from him as they became loosened with fresh blood and they crushed them upon the floor under their boots. One of the dark guards gripped the dwarf's hair and held his head back while his chin was cut bare under careless strokes of the other elf's razor. He screamed out so that his voice was echoing back to him, but no other dwarven cry returned to his ears, no whimper of another prisoner, no sounding of a heroic warrior, there was nothing calling back to him. A tear fell from his injured face as the sounds of his screams ceased echoing within the Iron Park for he knew that the wicked general had been right, that he was the last dwarf still alive within the city.

"You can be spared this unnecessary pain," however Hissilanda did not reveal any displeasure for committing to the torture. She remained focused only on the question, "Where is the path? Tell me where it is."

"It is the Stone Way," he tried to say through his teeth clenched by the pain. "A secret pass in the south of Dwamaklad. It is hidden in the cliffs."

"How do we see it," the queen leaned to hear through the wounded rasps of the dwarf lord.

"It is shown like the mountain, an illusion of Helena, but it reveals itself as you arrive at the head of the trail." He shivered as the cold metal of the knives touched his skin. "East! That pass is due east of the Iron Gate."

Hissilanda shook her head and the elves released the dwarf lord to the cobble stone of the crossroad in the iron Park. "There," she said calmly. "Now you can be released from this pain. It is a mercy that I give to you."

"Mercy?"

"To die now would give you time to reconcile with your demise," her smile faded and a deep sadness was in her eyes. As the dwarf lord looked up at her from the ground he saw the emotion linger for a moment and her brow became a wild anger at the sight of him. She gently waved her hand and one of her silver guard moved quickly to slay the dwarf as painlessly as possible as she had requested from the gesture.

"What did he tell you," Agnithia hissed in their language, her dwarvish worth little to keep up with their conversation.

"I have discovered the secret road to Arrumklad. I will be riding out with the armies to Presons."

"What of the Sentinel Woods? What are my warriors to do?"

"Have you begun to destroy the Iron Keep?"

"We have waited for your coming," Agnithia said. "The secrets that you wanted to learn may not have been offered by the dwarf you intended to keep."

"I suppose that this is a fortunate occurrence." Hissilanda scolded the general with her eyes, "But do not worry of things I have not labored you with."

"Yes, my queen."

Hissilanda looked into the upper terraces of the iron dome where the dwellings of the nobles remained untouched. "There must be a library in this keep. A dwarven trade lord would do well to amass information useful to their city hub. I assume it will tell of lineage and trade, though there may be texts of secrets we have yet to discover. Seek the information, along with any locations, supply sizes, and returning goods of the other dwarven holds. We must be thorough; every village, every mine, and especially every dwarf along the way will be dealt justice."

Agnithia turned and pointed to her personal guards, "Do you know the dwarven script?"

"Yes, Lady Witch-Heart. A few of us can read it. We will raid the library for the queen's answers."

"Go," She waved the guards away to their mission. "Will I still go to the east, my Queen?"

Hissilanda pushed gently on the back of the white stag and turned the creature toward the northern gate of the Iron Park. "Go when this city is erased, and go only with what you need. I shall take the rest of the allied forces to my calling." Hissilanda looked at the dark servants around her general. "Begin again at Argenkul. Destroy all who are there and along the way. You may have those towers when you are done, as promised. When you have finished there commune with me. We are not done yet, you and I." Queen Hissilanda the White began to ride northward while the armies beyond the courtyard of the Iron Keep gathered in ranks along the street to join her march and follow behind their queen once she had passed. She turned over her shoulder before leaving into the inner ring of the city, "Great work, Agnithia. I will consider your success when we deal with each other again."

Hissilanda began to lead the army down the Marching Road toward the north gate of the city and one of the chiefs from the tribes of Aelum'Hau arrived in her path to kneel before her. "Great queen, the lands of my ancestors are wide and will seek to lead outsiders astray. Allow me to go beside you and guide your path through the lands."

"With haste, Chief Selo'Hema of the Great Plains," Hissilanda invited the noble plainer elf within the sanctuary of her silver guards. "We will need to travel quickly and silently. No dwarf may be allowed to pass or speak amongst their holds of what has happened before we can act. We will fail if the secrecy of this war is lost and they raise their defenses against us."

The chief led the way through the northern gate and with a prayer hidden in song the plume of smoke began to shift as the wind altered course. The queen nodded to a silver guard beside her and they took up a curved horn which called all the elves to move onward at her command. Horn calls answered from all the districts of the city to rally to the queen. A massive force, larger than any host to have moved through the city of Ovelclutch before it, issued forth and then maneuvered away from the Marching Road into the vast grasslands toward the west. From the forest of Krethnarok, the queen's soldiers delivered new flags to the allied warriors. The nomads of the plains raised the flags with pride, the green tapestries of the Twin Rivers were gladly exchanged with the queen's banner, and even the black banners of the Sentinel Woods which remained in the city were replaced with silver tasseled flags of white. Together the elves moved on from the destroyed city of Ovelclutch toward the northern lands of the dwarves.

Agnithia waited in the central keep of the city while her servants and guards raided the upper levels of the Iron Keep. The dark shaeman stood beside her, silent until the last of the elves unaligned to the Sentinel Wood had left with the queen's calling. Their face paint was still dark with accents of silver, but it could not hide the violence that remained on their skin. "We have kept our secrets for now, Agnithia. Our plans, and those of the queen of Krethnarok, are kept among ourselves, though the Lady of Secrecy warns of a lost soul that has slipped through our grasp."

"Only one needs to escape to hinder the machinations of both our plans," Agnithia hissed harshly. "How?"

"The undercroft," the shaeman answered. "There is a tunnel that was unseen."

"The dwarves did not think to use this for escape?"

"We discovered many hiding in passages within the vaults beneath the streets. Perhaps they had thought that this was their safety."

"How did this lone soul escape the eyes of your servants?"

The shaeman closed their eyes against the general's insinuation of this failure, "The Lady of the Moon is not always forthcoming. Her secrets are offered should she be pleased, or perhaps we had not considered asking the right questions."

Agnithia considered what question to ask the dark shaeman, "Who escaped?"

"It matters not, for the risk is negligible. Their path wanders in the way of the queen. If it is not her that destroys this wanderer, then it will be the plains themselves, for this lone soul is a foreigner among elf kind."

"Then let us not be fooled again by these under-tunnels. Discover their purpose and be ready for such lairs. Argenkul is sure to have passages that run deeper than any within this city, and should we be needed again by the queen, the deepest paths of Helena's Cradle will test our expertise with dwarven secrets."

"Our forces are still strong and we will be keeping the bold one from the Twin Rivers for our plans. The dark moon is still watching. When we take the tower peaks you will have no need to worry any longer."

Agnithia hissed, "There is still much to worry while we have yet more dealings with the White Queen of Krethnarok."

CHAPTER III
THE DIGARDI

"Da, have you seen Kate?"

"No, Sarah." He was in the manor courtyard lifting heavy bundles of wheat onto a cart ready to head north into deeper Dwarf Country. "Your sister Katherine must have eluded you again."

Sarah frowned and thought to ask, "Have you seen William?"

Heaving another large bundle of harvested wheat onto the cart, her father stressed to say, "Yes I have." He laughed as he looked at his daughter, "Clever as always. He was in the barn last I saw." He pointed out to the large wood barn a good distance from them across the fields. "Don't tell him it was me who told you where to find him, love. The young ones would be devastated." He turned and lifted the last bundle of wheat onto the cart. "I need to go to the barley over near Swift Creek, sweetheart. Once this gets done we get paid for the season and you can be back on your way again."

Sarah smiled wide after hearing the good news and she turned to head out of the courtyard toward the barn.

"When you do find your youngers, come on back home. I may be out late and I need you all to help your mother tonight."

"While you are away, will you think much more about what I told you?"

"I will. The necklace you brought has been helpful I think, but taking your brother all the way to Bogramville, it's a heavy thing to consider." He brushed away the troublesome topic and gave her a big hug before getting into the driving seat behind the oxe. "Go off now. You'll miss us again soon when you go back to the city. Get it in while you are here."

She nodded eagerly and took off with haste towards the barn. It was cool in the manor courtyard under the shade of the old oak tree, but out in the fields it had become very warm beneath the open sun. Sarah did not try to show discomfort despite wearing the heavy red cloak of a mage scholar, instead she took the edges of it to billow out as she moved. She looked around at the raised plots just outside the manor wall and all around were crops of herbs that her father had planted for her return from the city. She grinned up at the sun and tried to identify the plants by their smell on the breeze.

As she began to near the barn her skip lessened to a stroll and she looked across the vast fields that were now emptied from harvest. The thought of following her father's footsteps into farming had always haunted her, but as she looked back at the manor from the barn she could see the entirety of her garden untouched by the field hands. She pinched the pendant at the end of her necklace and spun it in her fingers. It was the Eye of the Mage, a symbol of the Mage's Temple made in copper, and it restored her faith in her choices. She was excited to get back to Imitheon where she was studying herb lore at the city's Mage's Temple. It was a dream to open an apothecary, and with what she had learned already she was nearing such goals.

Sarah shook all of the day dreaming from her head and took hold of her necklace. She gave herself a final billowing lift of her cloak before letting go of the anticipation and she rounded the large doorway into the barn. It was wide open, an issue Kate had been given consequences for too many times already. To the left were stacks of hay bales, some stacked as tall as six heights, and to her right in stables were the three cows pulled in from pasture, each silently chewing from the troughs.

"Will?" She then called out with a frustrated sigh, "Kate?" A hush came from the loft above and an awful scuffling could be heard as the two attempted to hide more so than they already were. "Come down."

No reply came as the scuffling suddenly stopped.

"Please come down, I've already found you up there."

A giggle erupted and was quickly hushed by the other as though they had yet to be discovered.

Sarah rubbed the entirety of her face with exasperation and immediately fixed her hair that was already set perfectly in place. Slowly, not to be sneaky, but with the heavy movements of an already waning patience, she grabbed hold of the ladder leading up into the loft. Nothing stirred. *You have to go up there,* she ordered herself. Each rung took a long time to traverse, each step another futile attempt to let them come down on their own. As she neared the last rung both of the children sprinted out. Sarah reached out to try and stop them both, but it didn't slow either of them down.

William was quickest and he ran to the hay bales stacked near the height of the loft. He was the youngest, covered in dirt as he always was, but his feet were sure as he leapt down each step of the hay tower. Next came Kate. Her messy hair was pulled back into a long ponytail that was tied with a bit of ribbon that was too dirty to recognize as valuable cloth. She wore a dusty workers shirt meant for a small man and old dirty pants that were fitted with a cracked leather belt, each and every piece of the outfit giving way to heavy wear by her constant shenanigans. Kate did not have a plan, as was often the case, and suddenly unsure of herself, she stuttered a start towards a dangling rope before deciding to turn toward the haystack.

Kate leapt out to the hay bale tower but took a clumsy misstep. Horrified, Sarah watched as Kate hit one bail after the other and was flung to the ground after being tossed about. Sarah shouted and attempted down the ladder to rescue her sister, but she could not find the strength to break away from her shock.

William stood at the door, "Come on, if we get home first she can't catch us for chores."

Kate lifted herself up without hesitation and began to run passed her brother, "Well come on then."

Sarah's shock wore away and the frustration fully returned, "That isn't a rule!" As she stepped off of the ladder they were already nearing the outer garden of the manor courtyard. She sighed, closed her eyes, and enjoyed the quiet of the barn for a brief moment. A smile crept onto her face as she thought of her siblings, knowing full well that she at one time was just the same as them. She left the barn and began to head home in the evening sun, twisting the Eye of the Mage pendant between her fingers to reassure herself that she would be leaving for the city once again shortly.

As she walked along the path back to the courtyard, she caught the glare of a polished stone in the dust. "William," she sighed as she plucked up the item with concern. It was a gift that she had brought back from her time studying, a stone with a dwarven rune etched into the face and then polished for jewelry. It was strung onto a leather band as a necklace, but it had come undone from her brother's neck where it seemed the band had snapped. She hastened her step again and entered the courtyard, calling out for her brother who was hiding again.

"I will do the chores then," she begged. "Just come out here."

He slid down from the trunk of the old oak, "All of them?"

"Of course," she said kindly. "Just come here and put this back on."

William took it and Sarah made sure that the new knot was tight before putting it on over his head.

She hugged him and reminded him, "Dwarf runes are for good luck. You wouldn't want to ever take that off."

CHAPTER IV
THE BLACKROOT ARRIVING

The two assassins at last found the road through the grasses. Lilium peered north and could see that the mountain range that had guided them along their route began to dwindle into lesser foothills until it faded away entirely into the flat landscape of the grasslands. "We are nearly back at journey's start," she said to Terica, pointing at the mountain range northward and westward which was full of the green woodlands of their forest home of Krethnarok. "Hopefully our task can be done soon."

Terica knelt down and took notice that the grass refused to grow on the wide flat path before them. "What road is this?"

"The Marching Road," Lilium answered harshly. She pointed toward the south where the road cut straight through the nomad's grasslands toward the horizon, "The Empire of Man lives in their lands far to the south of here, but their roads seem to stretch beyond their sight easily enough."

"I thought the Empire was near to our home?"

"The Empire of Man also has territory in the north. They call it the Midland. The road here guides them between the two, but today it will guide us."

Terica looked down the road and followed it with her eyes northward beyond the foothills of the dwarven mountains and then passed the southern borders of the forest of Krethnarok. "Lilium, what is that?"

"Smoke," her eyes strained to focus at it in the distance. "A plume gathers."

"What lies there?"

"A dwarven city." Lilium stepped toward the north and waved her companion to follow. "It is not a friendly smoke either."

The two moved quickly, the road flat and even, the way free of debris or unsavory texture, and it guided them through the land without them needing to think of direction or obstacle. With haste they managed northward through the morning and midday, passed the paths toward the dwarven mountains to the east and their elven homeland to the west. Late into the evening they arrived at the southern gate of the dwarven city.

"Wide open," Terica noted.

"Torn open," Lilium corrected. "Elven arrows."

"The elves did this," but as they entered the city all around them were elves. They had white banners held high, though the warriors were all in dark garb.

"Sentinel elves did this," Lilium's eyes darted around to see who all could be around them. "Keep your guard high. These are cultists of a darker god."

"They have the white banners of the queen of Krethnarok, Hissilanda."

"Perhaps this was a bigger plan than just the Inland Sea could gather." Lilium led them into the narrow streets and all about were elves in dark garb searching every quarter to hunt the last of the dwarves' effects. At crossroads everywhere were pyres on which the victims were gathered and burned. Dwarven artifacts, books, images, and all else that could burn were brought out to the fires and the smoke rose over the city towers into the sky. Terica followed and they watched as the city was torn apart to the foundations and beneath in tunnels that were once hidden.

"Is this the first battle?" Terica looked at one of the piles and could see the glowing of metal armor as it melted in the fire's heat fueled by gathered material from the dwarven smithies. In the midst of the burning pyre was a dark patch that did not burn and it appeared to be the scales of a dragon that had been pressed into a jacket made of leather.

Lilium nodded, "There will be more bloodshed. Victory here will only drive the elven army's fervor."

"There weren't any nomads in the south grasses," Terica realized.

"I thought we were moving quietly," Lilium jested. "Perhaps this is more than just Krethnarok and the Sentinel Woods. I don't remember wood elves and plainer elves getting along well enough that they would call on each other like this."

"We could ask Vanessa, perhaps. We could go back to the Blackroot grove and-"

Lilium interrupted, "We still have a target to consider. Vanessa would have told us about this war if she meant for us to know anything."

"Is this perhaps what Vanessa was trying to warn us about?"

Lilium considered the wisdom from her companion, "Perhaps."

They continued through the streets toward the central keep, avoidant of other elves. "The easiest way through the city is straight across," Lilium directed. "We will get back onto the main road and get through the iron dome to the other side. If there is anything to discover it will be in that fortress. From there we find the north gate and maybe we can figure out the next path from there."

Terica nodded and they both continued in silence towards the Iron Keep. They entered the central courtyard between guard patrols and stood where shimmering rainbows now dazzled in cruel hues beneath the smoke. From the Iron Park they could see down every road in all directions, to the farthest districts of the city and all around were collections of the large pyres. With a silent wave of Lilium's hand they managed across the large mall between guards and warriors unnoticed. They lurked around statues and pillars, avoiding sight, and they kept an eye out for any leadership in the upper floors of the massive dome structure.

"Lilium," the whispering metallic voice came from the heart of the inner keep.

"Agnith," the Blackroot stood up from hiding and found the masked general standing in the center of the crossroad facing toward her. "Hiding from the sightless was unexpected."

Agnithia laughed at the teasing insult as she neared the two assassins from her position at the very center of the Iron Park. The other elves around her became aware of the Blackroot and whispered to each other what to do in case the assassins decided to attack. The personal guards of Agnithia drew their weapons, but she ordered them to stand down. "The Blackroot are honored guests to this victory."

Terica remained quiet while Lilium remained calm and confident. "The Blackroot were not aware that we were at war, though I am not surprised that the queen would use your skill to lead the attack."

From beneath the metal mask, Agnithia made harsh whispers at the pair of assassins. "Are you here for important targets then, or leads to such things? I may have already claimed your prizes," she gestured to the crushed jewels of the Trade Master that still littered the courtyard floor.

"We may be too late then," Lilium looked over her shoulder to Terica while scanning the upper floors for the dark servant she knew was hiding nearby.

"Certainly Vanessa would not charge you with pruning a lowly trade dwarf," Agnithia prodded. "Your goals are much loftier than only that. Have you at last come for me?"

Lilium's head spun quickly back to the metal mask of the elven general from the Sentinel Woods. "You are too close and too alive for that to be the case, Agnith."

"Perhaps the Blackroot are joining with the rest of us then. All of the other kingdoms have joined the radiant queen in her war."

"We move silently, but we are of like mind to elf kind," Lilium grinned, hoping to reveal as little as possible to the faceless adversary.

"Your kind might be joined back into the normal fold like mine if you prove yourself loyal. The light of the White Queen might grace us all."

"Where must we go to seek her out? Her army will move quickly, but if we get heading we can outpace them, just us two."

"Northward and westward, toward the woodland of Presons, but my own elves under my charge move to siege the next city, Argenkul, which is southward and eastward."

Lilium stepped back and placed a hand on Terica to move toward the north gate. "Then we Blackroot move northward and westward."

As the assassin stepped back the general stepped forward, now curious of any deceptions. "Since when do the assassins of the Blackroot involve themselves with the affairs of politics and military?" Agnithia came close, "Except when their purpose is such."

Lilium stared back, but the mask was difficult to intimidate. "Since when have moon cultists offered their service to the queen?"

"Loyalty drives us."

"An interesting answer given your own-"

"To the queen," Agnithia corrected the thought before the Blackroot could utter any blasphemies.

"Then you wouldn't suggest that the Blackroot lack loyalty." Lilium stood very still and Terica could feel the assassin's nerves quivering in the palm of the hand laid against her.

Agnithia suddenly bowed, "They moved northward and westward."

Lilium accepted the gesture and bowed back, "And you move southward and eastward."

As the pair of Blackroots moved to depart the Iron Park toward the northern gate, Agnithia seemed to stare. The elven general rose her voice so the harsh whisper beneath the mask stretched to rasping, "Safe travels through the grasses. Even the White Elf needed a guide."

CHAPTER V
WITCH HUNTING

It was a grim midmorning as the heavy mists of the Crab Bay gathered to hide the sun, the gray clouds were swept southward on the wind over the distant hills, and beneath the dim sky arrived the witch hunters to follow their prey. At the peak of the rise stood an Imperial Border stone, the designation of the end of the Empire, and beyond were the lawless lands. It was a large gray stone with four flat sides, bare of mosses, and it was placed upright so that it towered over the pair at twice their height. On the face of the stone by which they came was carved in the common tongue of the Empire, *'Beware, for our gaze enters not in these lands.'*

"It will do little to stop my own gaze, sister."

"Do not be too bold, Evelyn. These are Wilderlands. They have been abandoned and forsaken since the *Great War*. There may be worse dangers than our charge in this region."

"If so," Evelyn gripped the hilt of the great blade upon her back.

"Come. The trail continues this way."

"Always so focused on the hunt, Alison."

They crossed over the border and moved northward and westward into the Wilderlands. The two were on the Great Peninsula, a place west of the proper borders of the Empire, and lost across the rugged landscape were the ruins of old, littered amongst the hills and dales. Stray mountains and valleys pocked the lands as though the very earth paid little attention to this place during the creation of Nhearn's foundations. Amidst the rises and ravines were all types of tree, at times solitary and lonesome, and in other places the groves were so densely packed there was no passage at all between them. Water bubbled out from nearly every rocky crag and the springs gathered into pools that trickled into streams to form the many nameless rivers which carved the Wilderlands only more wild.

Alison and Evelyn moved on from the incredible sights, trekking deeper into the unmapped region. "Evelyn, I see something odd in the trail. It is old now, perhaps as old as a few months. I would guess that they were made during the last spring." They both knelt to view the odd grasses that were no more than the height of their knees. "Calcifor said we must be swift when we strike at this one." In the shape of a footprint, the grass was growing taller than the blades around it, the stalks were thicker, and the seeds much larger. "This plant cannot sustain itself. It withers in places, and see here," Alison wrenched the plant up from the soil. "The roots are normal."

Evelyn inspected it herself. "It cannot feed itself. Does it not grow all at once?"

"Perhaps if our charge had stood here for long enough then it might have grown more evenly. Calcifor said the witch's power was hazardous. Perhaps she radiates a cancer."

"He usually says it's dangerous," Evelyn scoffed. "I prefer hunting the ones that spit fire."

"I am sure there will still be dangers yet. We are the fourth hunter attempting this pursuit."

Evelyn stood tall and smiled confidently, "Who was the first?"

"A neophyte, nameless."

"The second?"

Alison looked the other huntress in their silver eyes, "I am too busy to remember the names of other hunters."

"The third then?" Evelyn's smile turned into a curled grin.

"I hope the witch affects your head, dear sister." Alison stood up from the bloated grass and her own silver eyes darted about through the scenery. "Seems the way has been gifted to us," she pointed deeper into the vegetation going eastward and set before them were odd patches of unmanageable growth that were in the shape of fleeing footprints. Both hunters followed the path at a quick pace, further into the Wilderlands.

Most of their trail was uphill, and the vegetation became more contorted with odd tumorous growths that held heavy on the boughs of the trees around them. A thicket of pine now blocked their trail to the summit of a sharp stone hill. A creek of clear water seemed to be the only way further toward the summit and it gleamed silver as the gloom of coastal clouds began to break apart in the afternoon sun.

Alison looked uphill and she could see the creek gently flowing from over the lip of the summit's crest. It flowed straight down a granite face in a shallow trench that the stream had carved for itself in the stone. The waters flowed into the creek between two walls of pine trees that lined the top of the hill like a crown, the trunks of them growing so bloated that they grew against one another and the wind itself could not pass them. "We may have just come to the end of our trail."

Evelyn's smile was wide and she began preparing herself for the fight ahead. "The witch will always trap itself in time."

Alison continued to stare at the pine trees and tried to calculate if they needed to worry of the growing curse themselves. "The witch must be afraid. It makes them more dangerous."

"Swiftly then," Evelyn tightened the belt straps of her armor, cinched the buckles down of the intricate steel plates, pulled taut her boot lacings beneath the sabaton attachment, and set her gauntlet locks before testing the joints in the fingers.

Alison became impatient; for her outfit had been prepared since they left their castle home of Tor-Torek and had not come loose, nor undone, as much as her sister's suit. "Ready?"

"Ready, sister," Evelyn said shortly, knowing the disappointment she brought upon herself.

In a tone that conveyed her dissatisfaction, Alison reiterated, "Swiftly?"

Evelyn nodded back and drew out her great blade. It was held heavy, even in both hands, and the metal of it shined purest black in the sunlight. Across the flat of the blade were rune markings, and in the silver hilt were embellishments of the Moon Goddess Aurora. In the center of the cross guard was a dark green crystal that hummed softly. Alison unsheathed her own blade that appeared as a twin to Evelyn's dark claymore.

They managed the incline through the stream and their boots clanked onto the bare stone as they went upward at a hasty pace. They came to the gap in the trees and the mouth of the creek was not bursting forth, but rather it seemed to flow from a gentle overfilling of the large pond that resided there. Around the pond, which had been slowly carved into a large bowl in the granite, was the wall of engorged pine trees. There was a deep silence there, serene and tranquil. It was a place fit for deep meditation. The only noise was at the far side of the pond where another gap in the tree line let water in from a stream which fed in as gently as the stream that flowed out.

"There," Alison pointed her blade to the pond's center and there sat a raft with a metal house built upon it which appeared to float on the water's surface.

"I just tightened my armor," Evelyn stated with exasperation as she peered into the water to check the depth.

"Swiftly doesn't mean recklessly. Swimming to the hut would be foolish." Alison pointed her sword again and Evelyn looked at the hut more carefully. It was made from a collection of rusting metal shields that must have been salvaged from one of the many ruins nearby. It was built upon a wooden raft, just wide enough to fit the hut, but it could do little against the weight of the shields to keep it afloat on the placid waters. "There is a shallow of rocks made on the other shore, I am sure of it." There was no doorway to be seen from their side, but a gap in the shields faced toward them like a narrow window. "What was your plan, sister?"

Evelyn could not see the bottom and the depth did not allow the afternoon sun to penetrate fully. It was too deep to cross and she sat down to begin undoing the straps off her boots. "Strip the armor weight, swim over to the hut, cut their head off, and leave."

"Reckless."

"It will work!"

Alison smiled for the first time on this trip, a glimpse that Evelyn was the only soul to see, for her sister was above all things stoic. "First to draw blood is the victor of this hunt then?"

"But you cannot swim, sister. I've already said my plan and you cannot have it. You will have to come up with your own way." Immediately Evelyn began taking off her armor more excitedly than she had been in tightening it.

"Fine," Alison began walking the narrow shoreline, a wide smile on her face as she became sure that she would be victorious. "Aurora guide your path, sister."

"Walk in moonlight, dear Alison," she replied, pulling the shell of her metal boot apart.

Alison continued around the edge of the water and found her balance challenged by the narrow bank of bare granite between the dark waters of the pond and the thick wall of the pine trees. At the edge set most between the two creeks she could no longer fit between the wall and ledge by the width of her shoulders. She quickly gave up on passing in silence as she struggled to stay out of the water and her metal boots clanked loudly on the bare stone for the effort. She inspected the pond and from where she stood she could now see that the creek coming into the pond had left a deposit of rock that gathered into a shallow embankment where one could walk over the pond to the door of the hut, just as she had predicted.

Evelyn, now weightless, with exception to the blade upon her back, went barefoot to the edge of the pond and waded in so that there was no sound or ripple. It was a quick drop off and all at once she could no longer stand. With her arms outstretched she gently paddled out into the water that darkened quickly beneath her.

Alison was nearing the creek on the far side as Evelyn neared the middle of the pond. Alison stepped into the flowing water and disturbed the trickling creek enough that a ripple formed on the placid pond. She saw the disturbance and then her foot was suddenly in a dry patch. The creek had stopped. Her head instinctively snapped toward upstream and staring at her was a gigantic bear. The creature's paw was so vast that it had dammed the creek wholly in its step. They locked eyes and through her silver gaze she could feel into its heart. It was afraid of her, but it was ready to defend this pit before it would dare to flee. She slowly lifted her sword toward it and the bear stood up on its hind legs in response. It was three times her height and she was already quite tall for a human. The serenity of the pond was destroyed as the bear roared and it did so more loudly than any bear ever had before it.

"You should have swam sister," Evelyn joked from the middle of the pond, no longer worried about hiding. As she began to break into a proper stroke toward the raft something touched her toes from the depths of the dark waters. It felt slippery, rigid in some places, it was strong, and solid too. It approached gently and vanished quickly. From beneath it rose up and touched Evelyn again on the leg, the gentle interest giving way into an aggressive beating from a heavy body that hit so maliciously it turned her back toward the shore. "Big fish," she tried to pull her sword from her back but she could feel that its weight in her hands would drag her below the surface. She gave up on grabbing the weapon and returned to treading water. "There are big creatures here, sister!"

"I have noticed." Alison stood her ground at the mouth of the stream and held her blade to impale the beast should it charge. The bear lunged before it fell onto its front paws and the ground shook under its crashing mass. As it rushed forward the muscles of the bear were plain to see and Alison knew this would be a proper test of her own might. The monster came down the incline of the creek at full speed and its teeth gnashed so she could see that its fangs were the size of long daggers. She stepped aside and the bear slipped into the pond as the deposited rocks from the inflowing creek rolled over the solid stone of the bowl beneath it. The beast turned with a snarling growl at the huntress who could see that her sister in the pond was also struggling to get closer to the hut and claim the victory from her.

From the darkest blue of the pond a shadow rushed upwards, and in a great splash, it leapt into the air beside Evelyn. It was silver in most places, deep red splotches were about it, and it had algae massed like drapery around it. From the corners of its gaping maw were great whiskers, and from dark eyes it seemed to watch Evelyn who was trying to stay at the water's surface.

"An eastern koi?" Evelyn managed well enough to stay afloat. "One big fish?" But as the giant fish was returning to the pond another creature came and crashed upon her legs. "Two big fish?"

The fish beneath her opened its maw wide and her foot was sucked inside. The monstrous fish bit down around her knee and it took her underwater. She tried to keep her eyes on the light of the surface, but her focus was taken by two swirling shadows above her. *Three big fish*. At her depth the sword would only guarantee death at the bottom, so she tried instead only to escape from the fish. She brought up her free leg and thrust down over the snout of the great koi. There would be bruising, but at least she was free from its grip.

Evelyn pushed upward and kicked about to speed herself back up to the surface, but in the water she was very much outmatched. The giant fish sped into her stomach and water whooshed through her ears until the koi breached into the sky. From the height she could see over the hut, see her sister and the bear, and she knew there was time still to reach the hut before her.

Alison had been avoiding the great bear's gnashing teeth and in her duel she had been driven over the shallow. As it lunged forward again, her sword plunged into the beast, and it knocked her prone as it trampled over her. The bank of gathered rock was only shallow enough that her mouth was above the water, but the bear was pushing her deeper into the loose stone and gravel. She retrieved a dagger from her waist and with the keen edge she slashed at the bear's arm. Blood spilled over the shallow and the monster began to move off of her. She gripped the hilt of her sword that still was held deep in the chest of the bear. As the monster retreated, it dragged her back onto her feet and she readied herself for another charge.

The brute growled and rampaged forward, but with clumsy speed Alison claimed the upper hand. She spun about and leveraged the sharp sword against the speed of the bear. The weapon struck true and the arm above the joint was cleaved from the monster. The gargantuan creature collapsed forward at full speed and cried out as it splashed into the pond. Alison took a breath before the bear began to recover and she could see that the fish were still whipping through the pond to give her sister a difficult time.

Evelyn had now been bitten twice, once more on the elbow so that her whole arm would bruise, and she had been launched from the surface once again. She quickly gathered the fish's behavior and prepared herself for another rush from below. A large koi came near and she struck it over the brow with her heel. As expected, the great fish dove and its shape flipped about to return against her at full speed. Evelyn bent at her knees and took the impact. The light of the surface came suddenly, but she managed her footing on the fish's snout well enough. She rose out from the pond atop the fish and Evelyn took flight off of the giant koi over the waters.

She had her blade ready in both hands, pointed downwards, and she watched her target below. As she flew over the pond, she shouted so that her sister might be able to hear her, "First blood!" *This is not going to be a pleasant landing.* Her target, a second fish which was possibly thinking of its youth and catching flies above the water's surface in sudden leaps, shot forth into the air, mouth agape, to swallow Evelyn. The tip of the blade caught the fish's scales between the eyes and the sharpness of the sword, along with the power from her flight, forced the blade in, all the way down to the silver hilt. Evelyn was rattled, thrown into the water as she took the brunt of the koi in flight to her body, and they both fell into the water that was becoming red with battle.

Blood now covered the shallow path also and the bear flung more blood about the shore as it thrashed with its wounded arm. With its one big paw it would lift up and swipe its claws at Alison. She stepped away from the hut, pushed onto the defensive by the monster, backing off the shallow in the pond and she stepped into the mouth of the creek on the shore. The bear would limp forward, swipe at her again, catch itself, and try once more. Alison waited, moved, waited, moved again, and when she could at last guarantee a moment to strike, she swung on the bear.

While Evelyn kept her blade sharp and true, Alison kept hers to a standard above, to a point of perfection. It was a razor at the edge, balanced a palm from the hilt, and though the metal was as black as a moonless night, it shined as brilliantly as any polished steel in the sun. It chopped over the hunch of the back, close to the neck, burying deep into the bone, and the bear fell to the ground. Alison pulled the blade out and it returned to her from within the flesh with ease. There was a deep bleeding gash in its back, but it seemed to do very little to halt the beast.

The bear rose up and its face snarled against the pain of its wounded shoulder. Alison gripped the hilt and grabbed her sword by the blade with her metal gauntlets, holding it confidently against the razor's edge as her gloves hid a thick metal slab against the palm. In both hands she placed the blade between her and the monster. The bear howled and opened its jaws to devour Alison. It fell upon her and the maw wrapped around the blade. Skin split at the corners of its mouth and Alison shoved into the monstrosity so that the blade ran deeper into the skull. The wet nose slapped her in the face as her arms held firm and the bear lurched forward. Its massive body went limp in the creek and blocked the gentle flow of water.

Alison wiped the blade clean on the matted fur before the beast's blood could dry and she looked to her sister who was still slashing wildly into the water atop the carcass of a giant floating koi. Alison was disappointed for a moment that she had lost and let it enter her tone as she got the attention of the celebrating huntress, "The other fish will eat the remains, sister. We have wasted enough time."

"Look at this," Evelyn shouted with enthusiasm. "The biggest fish. No port would dare call me a lesser fisherman for such sport as this."

"Even now, sister, your story is a bigger fish than you felled."

"It nearly ate me," Evelyn laughed. "And there were three!"

"They do not seem as contorted as the path grasses," Alison said with all seriousness in a hushed tone. "They have grown in size evenly, and in good health. The flora and fauna are all under the spell and have been so for some time. The witch is here." She turned her attention to the metal hut.

From the pond Evelyn lifted herself out of the water near the window, and from the shore Alison moved across the shallows toward the door of the hut. As they stepped onto the edge of the raft it sank slightly, leaning into the pond. It wasn't impressive, the wood planks must have been repurposed from a small cart, and if it wasn't situated on the last bit of the rocky deposit along the shallows it would not have remained afloat at all. "The witch is not a craftsman, it seems," Evelyn laughed at the shoddy hut.

Alison tightened the buckles of her gauntlets that had only slightly, but to her very noticeably, loosened in her fight, and she took up the hilt of her great sword to approach the door of the hut. Evelyn crept to the edge of the dwelling and crouched beneath the window as she wiped her wild hair back to get the water out from her sight. She took her sword and tested the grip for slipping.

Evelyn then guided the tip of her claymore between the shields while Alison took hold of the handle at the front door. Simultaneously the two hunters tore the hut apart. Shields that were strapped together with old rope and dried vines splashed into the pond with a ringing clatter. A beam of wood was all that remained of the structure across the raft and beneath a foraged table was a young woman curled in fear. Alison waved away hanging totems made from dry clay as she moved through the wreckage of the hut. "You have made yourself dwarven runes? Typical for one in your situation. This explains why my sword could not find you so easily. Sister, be careful that your sword does not strike them or the Dark Matter might ruin your blade."

"I know better than to do that again," Evelyn said before taking the frustration out on the table, tossing it aside and into the pond.

The witch looked up at Alison, her arms raised to cover herself in a useless defense against the witch hunter's blade. She was beautiful, youthful, and what remained of the tattered clothes showed that she had come from some level of Imperial prestige. "I have gone away," she said in a gentle voice. "I cannot hurt anyone here."

"Lies," Evelyn shouted. "There is no safe haven for a witch. You have no control of your power. The magic will swell in you again, and when it does, you will only be able to blame yourself."

The witch collapsed, trying to hide as much as they could. "I am nowhere now. I am outside of the borders! The Empire has no jurisdiction-"

"The Auroran transcend such politics," Alison interrupted the plea.

"Auroran," the witch looked up at her attackers and saw the moon symbols on their chests. They had glowing silver eyes that pierced into her soul and could see that she had already hurt people before she had fled into the Wilderlands. "Please, paladins, please don't kill me! I am not evil. Aurora, in all her goodness, she would never-"

"With what dangers you've created it would be unwise for the Auroran to leave you alive," Alison said as she stepped over the witch. In her grip the sword began to hum louder as it lingered above the girl and the dark green gem began to glow within the hilt while the witch became weaker beneath her presence. Alison stepped back to let her sister close in, "It is her."

Evelyn held her blade up to strike as Alison began an official statement. "For the dangers you possess and the involuntary crimes of your existence, Aurora has brought us here to complete your sentence. May you walk in moonlight, when at last your innocence has returned to you."

Evelyn swung and her sword seemed to take the noise from the air. The gem in the hilt glowed briefly with a sickly green ember and dimmed as the magic nearby faded away. "Walk in moonlight," she added coldly.

CHAPTER VI
ABNOGNE

Basimick had been left in the tall grasses of the Great Plains, but within his heart was a heading. He moved toward somewhere, only led on by a feeling that he knew the wind spirit must have gifted him. Basimick used his hands to separate the grasses along his route, pulling himself over bundles of thatch, and at last the grass began to dwindle in height. His head began to see over the tall fronds, after a few more steps his chest could now clear the canopy, and over a short distance more it fell below his knees.

Before him was a wide clearing that had been cut apart from the rest of the plains, and in all directions there was nothing more to see but the rolling waves of grass in the breeze all the way to the edge of sight. At the center of the clearing was a large dome, a large blue structure that was nearly three heights tall at its peak. Where the large thing was buried into the ground was a doorway that had been carved into the very center of it. The structure was wide and it swooped into spiked edges as though it were meant to look like the back of some massive crustacean. Dug into the ground around the blue dome and throughout the entire clearing were square pits that could fit a person inside. Some of the holes were shaded by large cuts of colorful canvas that had been stretched over scaffolding which was made from bundled grasses. There seemed to be many rooms made from the canvas structures, each one separated by curtains to offer more privacy to each pit.

He began to near the colorful rooms along a route where the grass had been trampled by repeated use heading toward the blue structure door. Around him were pits alongside the path, some empty which appeared like graves left uncovered in the sun. Basimick walked beyond the outer set of holes deeper into the clearing, and as he neared the pits that were dug closer to the structures he was surprised to find the holes filled with loose mud. Each of the filled pits were churning and boiling with clear waters that bubbled from springs below so that the waters settled across the top of the mud like a mirror. He continued toward the center structure, stepping along the path that turned and cornered around the pits which were becoming more numerous near the middle of the clearing. The path led him near a canvased room that was unoccupied. He was disappointed that perhaps the whole place was abandoned and that the wind spirit had carried him astray.

Basimick turned to look back over the horizon for a new direction, but his hand flinched toward his sword as he was confronted by an elf that had suddenly appeared behind him. They made no noise; instead they held their hands together over their chest and bowed to him.

"Who are you," Basimick asked the elf with worry.

"You have been guided here," they said cryptically in the common tongue.

"Where am I?"

"Nowhere," they said in a properly rehearsed fashion. "Welcome to Abnogne, by the graces you have come to the heart of the Great Plains. Allow us to soothe your woes."

"Soothe my woes?"

"All who are led here are led to be soothed. It is our gift, just as Vanessa would wish."

Basimick was frightened by the elf and as more came from within the domed structure he became concerned that they would learn he had come from Ovelclutch where the armies of elves had attacked. None of them bothered with where he had been however, and none of them bothered to ask why he was there, they simply went to work. An elf arrived with a large vase and offered him water that tasted sweeter than any he had ever tasted before. Another came to him with a flat tray who offered him food that was foreign to him, but it tasted like crisped bread and sweet grapes.

Basimick was worried, his thoughts racing as the elves hurried him near a pit where a pair of elves lifted the edge of a curtain and brought him into one of the canvas rooms to shade him from the open sun. Within the colorful room was a wooden bench that had a restful tilt toward the pit and there were also collections of clay vases which held waters, oils, and dried herbs that filled the space with a relaxing aroma.

The crew of elves vanished suddenly so that only a lone elf stayed and drew Basimick's attention to the bench with a pat of his hand. "Place your things of importance here," the elf said slowly to think of the right words in Imperial Common. "They will be safe from your worry."

He was hesitant to do so but could not think of a reason to avoid it. He was also afraid to upset any hospitality he was being given and the overwhelming feeling of belonging was clouding his judgment. He took the sword from his belt and gripped it tightly before setting it on the ground to avoid the elf's direction in case it would be taken away.

As his hand left the hilt on the ground, another elf came from under the curtain before kneeling with reverence to collect the sword from the ground. Basimick was quick to turn about and shout so that the elf retreated before they could touch the sword. They bowed their head and fell to their knees, repeating the same word again and again. They spoke in elvish and he was immediately confused, but the elf seemed genuinely upset by the insult he had given to Basimick.

"Place your importance here," the lead elf suggested again, now trying to think of words to explain. "This is Seh'ladu," the elf lifted their companion from their knees. "Seh'ladu can work the metal of the earth and can clean it to splendor," and then the elf pointed at the blade on the ground.

"No," Basimick said simply to avoid any confusion. "Thank you," he bowed to avoid seeming rude for the offer. He took up the sword and placed it on the bench while bowing, hands drawn together over his chest, toward Seh'ladu who bowed back before departing the room.

"What you leave down, we will mend," the elf said with a wide smile and pointed to the ground.

"I understand," Basimick nodded and tried to convey with his hands that he understood their directions. His boots were taken, and his jacket was picked up. He placed the three hunter's tokens on the bench and before he could place his empty satchel that was meant for food upon the bench the elf shook their head. Basimick's smile widened and he was happy to place the satchel on the floor to be filled with the delicious foods he was being offered.

He was exposed, but his sword was close by and nobody seemed to be threatening him or reaching toward the bench. The elf waved their hands to shoo away the others that had returned to the edge of the room with fresh offerings and everyone went off to vanish among the clearing to other duties. The elf then pointed to the mud pit and simply said, "In."

The mud bathes were wondrous and he fell into a slumber as the heaviness of it soothed his weary limbs. He had not relaxed since the end of the harvest last season and had far less opportunity now that he was questing about. He wondered where Cassius and Longinus had gone following the elven attack on Ovelclutch, but those thoughts were slowly wasting away from him as the mud soaked his core with healing.

The silhouette of another visitor rounded the curtains toward the edge of the room which he was facing from the bath. An elf with glistening oiled skin and green inked tattoos slowly lifted the curtain into the canvas room where they stood at the foot of the mud pit, waving gently to be sure that they got his attention so as not to cause any surprise. "How are we, young master," they said in common. "How does the bath feel?"

Basimick was relieved that all of the elves were speaking in his language, and he smiled lazily back at them. "It feels grand."

"This is good. Feel rested. Be at peace." The elf set a basket of woven grass on the surface of the bath and it rested on top of the churning mud while warm water bubbled toward the surface of the mud from within the earth."

"What is this," he stared at the basket and asked with a heavy effort.

"It cleans the spirit," the elf said. "A remedy from ancient times, one that has been passed down from my tribe lords and wise shaemans." The elf struck a rock over another so that a few hot shards, each one glowing with fires intent, cracked away and poured into the mud with wisps of white smoke. Basimick was alarmed, but he could not move away against the heaviness of the mud around him. He was thankful that the glowing shards all fell true into the basket. The elf struck it a few more times after the concern wore off of their guest's face and at last the basket caught the embers to be set ablaze. "Sacred grasses and pleasant flowers soaked with healing oils. The smoke will sit and calm you, master."

"Why do you call me master," Basimick asked hesitantly."

"It is to be respectful. Forgiven is the old way of man, for each soul is not of one mind or purpose."

"Thank you. That seems to be a hard lesson to learn," he thought of how fearful he had been that the spirit had carried him to the elves, but he was put more at ease by the words of his host.

"The eyes can see much of what is, and the heart can believe that what is is true of all." The elf nodded and fanned the blaze until it was extinguished so that only smoke rose from the basket embers as it slowly blackened into ash. "But this is a falsehood, is it not, master?" The elf then retired the tools to a vase nearby the pit, returned to the foot of the mud bath, and sat, pointing at the center of their chest as they did so. "I am shaeman to my people."

The shaeman's wicker basket was burning between them. Basimick sank into the mud pit and thought before observing the elf at the foot of the pit. They sat with their legs crossed and their hands together over their chest with their eyes closed. Basimick was relaxed and prepared to speak, but the elf already seemed prepared to interrupt him, "Why are you here?"

"I do not know. I didn't know this place existed. I was lost."

"Simple answers reveal the most truth. You do not know why you are here," the shaeman pointed to the ground. "This place knows." They took a deep breath and then centered their hands over their chest, "Are you alone?"

"Yes," Basimick answered simply, a somber sigh following.

"You and three others arrive today. It is strange that we receive so many who are so unrelated, each one alone in their own ways."

Worry drove his question quickly from his mouth, "Are they from Ovelclutch?"

"No. Do not be worried, this place is not aligned or mastered by others than ourselves. You have no enemies here." The shaeman opened their eyes and the heat of the basket rippled so that the air between both of their faces was warped. "Who brought you here?"

Basimick was silent and still as he attempted to recall details before his arrival. They were hazy memories. He recalled smoke and glow from Ovelclutch, tall grass, no shade, a breeze, and the wind. He remembered then, a strong wind at his back and the howling gale over the hills. The smoke of the mud bath smelled sweet and the shaeman's basket crumbled to ash on top of the mud. He remembered a monster, an elf, and the warnings of terrible things in the west. "E're thorbranni," he whispered, trying to recall the somber phrase of the spirit.

"O're ec thorbranni," the shaeman answered and shut their eyes with a smile. "Did the beast reveal itself to you? Perhaps it was a spirit or just the wind when you heard these words?"

Basimick closed his eyes and the wind in the grass was on his mind. It moved in and out, as if it were breathing with the world. "Hoopha."

"So it told you his name." The shaeman smiled, "You are meant to be here, young master."

"Who was he?"

The shaeman opened their hands in ceremony and they dangled their necklace to show to Basimick. It was a strange thing, a horror to wear. It was made of fingers that had been sewn onto a thick twine and none of the fingers seemed to belong to the same victim. "You are nervous, but you do not yet understand. Your people, those of the Empire of Man, they fear passing, but my people revere the thoughts of our ancestors, and they know that this is only the beginning of true freedoms." The shaeman pointed to a specific finger upon the twine, "This one is Hoopha, warrior chief who saved our people, as his forebear had done in the times before him. Aelum'Hau, greatest among the legends of the plains, was granted peace when Hoopha arose. The great chief was released to the other side where the great tower rests near to the realms of the sky, near the dominion of Katrina, where spirits can be lifted into flight upon her tune." The shaeman returned the necklace to its proper place about their neck. "Hoopha refuses to rest, for he believes he is not yet done with his purpose."

"He told me about a fire. He hopes he can hold it back somehow. Stop it from spreading into the grasslands."

"Victory against that fight will not come from Hoopha, though he may yet serve to help."

"Who is he?"

"I shall share with you the stories of my people." The shaeman smiled, but it vanished into a somber state as they rose to collect a new concoction from the ceramic vases. They took the flowers and dipped them into a vase full of oils. They wove the stems into a tight ring and whispered elvish into their cupped hands so that Basimick couldn't hear. The shaeman sat down at the foot of the bath and began to blow into their hands which caused an ember to burn as though an incantation of magic had occurred. They took in a deep breath and blew the rising smoke toward Basimick and as it struck his face the voice of the shaeman began to blur with visions of a distant place in a faraway time.

*****

Hoopha, chief of the greatest of the last tribes in the Great Plains, stood over the fire that lit the whole interior of the Meeting House in a violent glow. It was loud within the large space; echoes carried well in the structure and everyone wanted to be heard. The Meeting House was made from the very last greater crab, its shell hollowed and furnished to make a beautiful home. Hoopha, old enough to remember the time of the great crab hunts, took his pride totem that rested upon his chair beside the fire and aggressively let it loose into the flames.

Those gathered to meet with him were taken aback at the sudden fervor and sacrifice of the important artifact. "Look at us!" Hoopha took hold of a warrior's spear and guided the point of it at the leaders around him, each one visiting from distant paths of the plains. "Fallen Tribes!" He shoved the tip into the fire and sparks of crashing embers filled the room like they were angry ember wisps. "We have hunted the great crabs of old! We have learned of the grass and the field! We have driven out a hundred enemies! This is our home," Hoopha waited for the roars of the other leaders to dwindle as the excitement overcame them. "Yet we lose our lands to the Empire of Man."

Another chief stepped toward the glow of the fire and presented his totem before speaking, "The humans are too many and too zealous. They have captured my tribe members and forced them to build the towers."

"The humans cut down my warriors, chased down my hunters, and killed the others," said another chief who looked upon his pride totem one last moment before casting it into the fire. "Nothing is left."

"They came from the south, now nothing comes from the south. The great grass bison have vanished, the panthers do not roam, and even the carrion birds do not fly here any longer. We are starving, all of us who live near their roads now." The chief took hold of the first to speak and they tossed their pride totems into the flame together.

"One," Hoopha rapped the spear on the floor.

"One," the other chiefs answered him before each of the members tossed their artifacts into the fire which grew intense as the magic charms upon them returned to the air.

Hoopha undid the necklace and held it high to show it proudly among his kinsmen. "The finger bones of our forebears, our greatest leaders. They shall guide us!"

The other elves cheered and the Meeting House roared as the honorable shaeman of Hoopha's great tribe entered the glow of the fire. They approached Hoopha who bowed deeply with respect and the necklace he stewarded was offered to the spiritual leader. The shaeman rested their staff before continuing their inspection of the artifact. One by one, with hushed reverence, the bones were removed from the chieftain's necklace. Each one was the left pointer finger of the ancestor chiefs, and they were placed in order of their reign upon the necklace. As they were removed they were sorted by the shaeman to be placed onto a carved wooden board in order of their earned respects and the gratitude of antiquity.

"What do they say, Wise One?" Hoopha peered over the shoulder of the shaeman as they worked toward the fire in front of his presiding chair.

"Fear is not walking among our enemy. Confidence and arrogance, this is what makes them vulnerable. They are weak now, but they will grow in strength as we wane in numbers." The shaeman scooped all eight of the bones from the board and then dropped them with a whisper to Katrina for assistance in reading the secrets they would tell. The bones scattered about, but one struck the board harshly and tumbled into the hottest patch of ember within the bonfire. Some of the chiefs moved to catch it, but a swift wave of the shaeman forbid any action to hinder where it went. "Look, all of you, while he may yet linger with us. The advice of the second forebear directs us to act. Aelum'Hau, warrior chief of our lands, savior of the grasses, he points now to Hoopha!" The shaeman stood up from their crouched position over the bones. "It will be his final request before he joins antiquity. At last he will rest within the Tower and fly among the birds near Katrina."

Hoopha set down the spear and kneeled to face the fire. The finger pointed at him, and even as the fire cracked into sparks, the finger remained directed at him. "Rest upon the winds, forebear."

"Gales guide him to the songs of the greater winds," the shaeman prayed while the others in the Meeting House bowed their heads as the spirit of Aelum'Hau passed on. "Now, Chief Hoopha, we know where it is that you will rest in your time." The shaeman collected the bones and sat to thread the fingers back to their historical places upon the artifact.

At last, one of the chiefs asked of the shaeman, "Who is to help Hoopha?"

"It is a trial that he will face alone, as Aelum'Hau did when he was tested long ago."

Another spoke up, "What is he to do?"

"He will war," the shaeman answered gently.

"One alone against so many?"

"He is meant to be the one to decide our fates," The shaeman waved their staff into the smoke to send the chief of old onward. "As Aelum'Hau did in his time."

The shaeman gave Hoopha their staff and he found it was a great spear made from ivory chitin and armored plates of the great crab. The weapon was elaborately made, though the white of it had been left bare. It was a blank tapestry waiting for a story to be written upon it, for it had only been gaining magics in ceremony and ritual for the last few hundred years. Hoopha bowed to the shaeman and took it in both hands with great respect, knowing now that it was he who would weave the legend that was to adorn the creation. Hoopha removed the ivory cap and revealed a spear head made of polished steel. It was to become legendary; a historical artifact to pass down to the new faces of the plain elves beyond him, and it gave him hope.

"Take also the hunting mask," the shaeman said, pointing to the doorway of the Meeting House.

Above the door were three masks made of bone. One, set to the left, was the skull of a large horned grass bison, cleaned and bleached. It was decorated in its entirety with silver stripes over golden paints, and it had the furs of the grass panther braided through tooled holes to make a proper hood. It was the mask of beauty and was used during a half moon on a day where the chieftain's heir must claim their intentions or forfeit leadership to the next kin members.

Hoopha looked to the center mask which was set higher over the doorway than the other two beside it. It was also made from a skull, a wind drake, bleached also and striped with red blood from all the great hunted beasts of the plains. This mask was used for boons of leadership and power by the chieftains. It was worn with a black cloak in ceremony during a passing of leadership or when the shaeman would call upon the ghosts of the forbearers to answer the tribe on holidays of respect.

The hunting mask was far more horrific, and it rested to the right of the doorway beneath the mask of power. It was made from the skull of a large and skilled grass panther, bleached as the others were, but it was not at all painted. Instead it was rubbed with the ashes of crematory fires, fires that were made specifically under the prayer of a powerful shaeman to rest the souls of fallen enemies and this was especially the case for victories over heated rivalries. It was worn as a helm and the bearer's face was painted with pitch so that through the fanged open maw there was only darkness. The cap and adorning cloak were then made from the quills of fallen prairie sneaks, each barbed spike hand-picked from the thousands for their perfect translucent crystalline white color. It, along with a blood red leather cuirass, was worn to make the wearer into a true monstrous terror.

Hoopha wore these artifacts with pride. The confidence of the spear and mask showed as though a mystical aura had taken hold of him. Even if the other chiefs within the Meeting House had doubts, they refused to show it or speak up now that the shaeman had spoken. They all bowed before the fire and honored the guidance of their ancient leader as the finger bone crumbled to ash in the great fire.

"Go now with the hunt, mighty Hoopha," the shaeman bowed their head to the warrior, "and save these great lands of our people."

Hoopha only used enough time to grab a small satchel of food before he wandered into the Great Plains alone. Snow had been falling now in late winter and it made the land almost indiscernible, even for someone as familiar to the region as Hoopha. He was guided only by the winds and the spirits, and they did so gladly, leading him on his way for many days until he found a banner amidst the wilds. It stood all alone, driven into the snow, and the Empire's sigil was adorning it.

Afar was a single turret over the snowdrift plains, surrounding the tower was a high wall of stone, and from within the enclosure smoke rose from great fires lit to fight the cold. Hoopha crouched and the white quill cloak hid him as a winter beast. He closed his eyes to listen as the wind echoed through his skull helm, carrying with it the whispers of the spirits and their reason for his being there.

Shouts, whimpers, and cries for help. Not in the tongues of foreigners, but of the elven plain folk. The cracking of whips could be heard as well as the constant striking of metal on stone. *Enslavement*, he thought. It made him angry, but the mask seemed to harness and quell his rage, leaving only the focus and drive to accomplish his task. With unmatched haste he crossed a great distance and rushed toward the open gate of the small fortress.

Set in front of the gate were two shivering humans, each clad in Imperial iron armors, which would make them heavy on the snow. They held swords that had a shine to them, no chipping or wear, and Hoopha knew that their weapons had never seen battle or known violence. One of the guards peered through the harsh weather and shrugged away the fast moving thing as a wild fox, but the other saw the dark maw and ash covered helm. They nearly fell from fright before crying out, "Monster!"

The witness raised their undented shield, but the sharp whistle of Hoopha's deadly spear did not strike at them. A heavy thunk sounded and beside the guard his companion fell into the snow bank against the fortress wall, the ivory shaft of the chitin spear buried deep into his chest. A heavy blow suddenly knocked the shield from the remaining guard's hands. Before them was a terror and they watched with the eyes of a young child as the nightmare fell upon them.

Blow after blow struck the youth's head and chest, disorienting and then debilitating the guard. Hoopha crouched low and swept the legs out from under the Imperial. Through the fall, the elf warrior seized the hilt of his enemy's blade, and as the human hit the ground their own weapon stabbed them through the iron plate, into the gut.

Both guards felled, Hoopha took back the spear and leapt up onto the brick, hoisting himself to the ceiling of the gate passage into the fortress interior. There he waited to strike from above.

Several more soldiers arrived and spoke in a hurried panic. Two ran off to seek more help and the other three stayed to investigate the attack. Hoopha made a warrior's howl and leapt from his perch above them. Both hands on the spear, he fell upon the center soldier, driving the weapon all the way through them so that he could pull the weapon back to his control from the other side of his enemy. In their surprise they froze and Hoopha spun the spear about, striking the remaining two soldiers in the sides of their heads, knocking them both unconscious simultaneously.

A horn blew and the fortress became a noisy place with the shouts of foreigners. Hoopha crouched back into the snow and was hidden again. All about the fortress he could hear them use whistling weapons and hear their metal striking stones at a distance; aimless attempts to scare away what they thought must have been a wild creature that could be easily panicked. A dozen young humans rushed from the doorway of the turret and looked about to see if anything that was attacking them remained. None could spot Hoopha who looked like a drift in the snow within their own walls.

They went to the gate passage and discovered the bloody scene of their comrades' defeat. From there they made shouts for help, gasps of surprise, and cried out at the horror that had befallen them. As they rounded the outside of their own wall to see what could have done such a deed, Hoopha pounced at their backs. His spear cared not for their iron armor, his skill weaved around their clumsy attempts to strike back at him, and the relentlessness that Hoopha wielded ensured that none would leave this battle alive.

He hated them all, but his hatred did not lead his hands. It were as though the mask held his rage and focused it into a graceful dance where victory was entirely certain. A dozen imperial bodies laid about him, but he was not exhausted in the slightest. With all the speed that he had, Hoopha went back into the fortress courtyards where his people were forced into servitude. They mined for stone and clay beneath the conquered hills of their own land to build more walls and towers for the foreigners.

The head of the great spear cracked over their chains like a bolt of Katrina's lightning and within moments all his brethren were free from their shackles. One of them looked at what the Imperials had called a monster, but they could see that it was a wind spirit, a helpful and friendly thing to those who knew it. They did not cry or shout, instead they bowed in thanks, but as their gaze left the sight of the helpful spirit, Hoopha vanished. He drifted into the grasslands, as though the wind carried him, and his stride was untraceable through the snow of the Great Plains.

*****

When the story had ended, Basimick began to wake. The ash of the basket was scattered by the breeze and laid thinly dispersed over the warm mud. He strained his eyes and struggled to think if it were all just a dream or the vivid imaginings of real events. The shaeman was gone, but the day was still bright. He had not drifted away for long at all.

He leisurely looked at his things, the comfort of the bath sapping him of effort. On the bench was set his blade and the tokens. Beside these were his cleaned boots, his clothes, and a satchel that was filled with fresh wonders of the foreign pallet. Truly the generosity and genuine good nature of this place was gifted to him as if by magic. It was enough that his fear of elves was drawn away and he could think clearly of Hoopha for a moment.

There was no ending to the shaeman's vision, but Basimick had felt the emotion of the chief, felt the grief and rage that had overcome all of the elves of the plains. He peered about the pits of Abnogne to see if any of the assistants were near him, and as he did, he realized that he had thought much the same about elves after the attack on Ovelclutch, much as the elves had done against the Imperials in their time. His eyes then wandered to his father's sword and he wondered if the shaeman's story might have been about the loneliness that Hoopha endured, much that he now endured. His mind wandered to a thousand meanings of the story; that he was one of the foreigners trespassing, or that the elves no longer felt this resentment and would feed him their delicious food as equally as they would to elves, or that perhaps he knew nothing at all.

He rested back into the mud and found that his arms no longer ached, that his legs were free of pain, and the shivers he once had no control over had vanished. Basimick slumped back into the mud pit when a voice from nearby jolted him from his thoughts, "It is a wonderful place, is it not? The baths of Abnogne are hard to find and lost to maps. Not many could ruin the solitude."

Basimick was more startled by the stranger's voice than when he had been approached by the crew of elves. "Who is this?"

"I am next to you, too relaxed to move any myself. I'm easily missed as it were. My name is Tydas and I am a wanderer. You must also be a traveler to come so deep into the uncharted places of Nhearn."

"My name is Basimick," he said. "I have no home now and I think I am running from a great many things."

There was a silence and at last Tydas said, "I suppose luck could bring you here as well."

Tydas rested into his bath, a bit upset that his beard was crusting with the thick clay, but the warmth of the churning mud around him washed away even this worry. "Master of light," the shaeman called to him as they entered the curtained room from the foot of his pit. "Let the child rest longer and think of my lessons, I must speak with you."

"Yes, honored one."

"Always a pleasure to be your host. How fair thee on your travels?"

"Well, thus far," he relaxed deeper into the mud at the presence of the shaeman. "Southrunn is well, worried for the orc, but it seems that the world is these days. Tronia is well, though no news south of there so long as you are aware of the Black Mountain issues."

"Christianna guides you well?"

"As Vanessa bless you and Katrina guides you." Tydas looked at his hammer resting untouched beside the bench. It was a heavy sledge with polished embellishments displaying depictions of Heaven and angels. In the center of every face was the double iron cross of Christianna, polished and bright. The pole that the holy hammer head was affixed to was steel and at its end was a spike that he had driven into the ground so that the whole weapon stood upright. The top of the hammer was wide and flat, and upon it he kept a small Christiannan book of prayer. The way it rested beside the bench made it unrecognizable as a weapon and its purpose seemed to resemble more of a traveling altar.

"You are weighed heavy, Tydas," the shaeman set a basket filled with a bouquet of colorful flowers into the mud bath and set the edge ablaze with an elven incantation. After a moment they used a fan of reeds to blow out the fire and the smoke of embers released a calming aura within the curtained room.

"Heavy, yes. I am going north to meet with someone about something troubling, I believe." He looked at the resting book and gestured for the shaeman to see it.

Inside was a letter bookmarked on a prayer of meeting. "This letter is from Elminil White-Waters?"

"The Elminil," Tydas confirmed.

"My grand forebears spoke of him. Does he not yet rest?"

"Christianna and Aurora will weep on such a day." Tydas waited for the book and letter to return to their place atop his hammer. "I wonder why he would call for me though, he being so far north and I being so far south. We have never met, though I have heard of his name passing in rumor and lore."

"If your name would not be shared the same as his you should fear your church, Tydas. Aurora would wish you for her purposes if she could find a way to convert you from the Daughter of Gold."

"I am not strong enough to want a moonlit path. Kindness and goodness are all Nhearn needs."

"Perhaps that is what Elminil hopes for when he sees you."

"That is good insight," Tydas closed his eyes as the smoldering petals sank him more into the mud with rest. "I would like to hope that is his desire."

The shaeman stood up and bowed. "Rest, Tydas of Light. I fear that darkness is coming and we will need your spirit."

Basimick waited for Tydas to begin speaking again, but the area went quiet and he thought to leave Tydas to his own thoughts. After a few moments the smell of the burning petals struck his own bath and the aroma removed what little tension there was left in Basimick. The shaeman left, their shadow passing over the curtain of his room, and he was left alone to continue thinking about the dark history of the plains, why Hoopha had allowed a human to cross his lands, or what any of it meant for him.

CHAPTER VII
THE BLACKROOT IN ABNOGNE

The pair of assassins wandered into the clearing from out of the grasslands. They did not appear fatigued and they carried so little that they were not met by any of the elven crew. Lilium could see that there was already a gathering of rooms built near one side of the central blue meeting house. Assuming that they were not the only visitors to the sacred place, she led Terica down the trodden paths to more distant mud baths to isolate themselves. "Vanessa has led us here again," she smiled at Terica.

"I do enjoy this respite," Terica laughed. "It makes the walk bearable."

They went to the distant bath pits, but Lilium was disappointed to find that they were emptied of the healing clays. Shovels and ceremonial pots to gather the healing mud were strewn about the area and her eyes followed a light trail of mud drippings which led toward the freshly filled pits. "I suppose we will have to join whatever company has found their way to the hot spring."

"There are so few who would come. I do not believe that the White Elf or any other of her kin would even know of such places."

"Best to be on our guard still," Lilium whispered. "I don't want anything to happen to the vile blade."

"The shaeman will make sure that we are well attended at least. No one would dare bother another in the sacred baths of Abnogne."

"Especially Blackroot," Lilium smirked.

The pair went to the colorful canopy shades and tried to find what baths they could. Terica discovered that the first room was unoccupied. She entered by slipping around the side of the curtain to avoid making much motion and she maneuvered out of her belongings quietly. She set both of her Blackroot blades upon the bench before slowly sinking into the pit without the assistance of an attendant. As the mud began to soothe her she sighed, hoping it was loud enough that the elves of Abnogne could hear that she had arrived.

Lilium continued on the path, passing several of the colorful rooms before she discovered an empty pit and she opened the curtain to the unoccupied bath. Her eyes darted around, but no shadows were casting their silhouettes on any of the canvas walls around her. Lilium took her time to enter the soothing bath and as she entered the thick healing clay the shaeman entered the room. "Unusual custom to be greeted by you before your tribesmen."

The shaeman looked at the bench, "These are unusual times."

Lilium's only items on the bench were her own two blades in the ceremonial Blackroot style and set apart was the dreadful blade wrapped in unassuming cloth. All else was upon the floor, though it was not much to be traveling by. "Do not touch it," Lilium stated. "You have come to me too soon. You can sense something and I know what it is that you are feeling."

"I do not think so," the shaeman sat at the edge of the bath and centered themselves before talking to the assassin. "I am worried, for what you have brought here is wicked and untamed." The shaeman glanced toward the other rooms, but then they shook their head at their wandering thoughts. "But what troubles me most is the sense of a great and oppressive weight upon you. Such a thing is not as rare as I would hope, it seems." The shaeman crushed sprigs of dry lavender over the mud in attempts to soothe the wood elf slightly. "Such weapons as these are artifacts of an ancient hate. It takes a true sense of innocence to guide them properly."

"You believe that I am not capable?"

"Is that what you worry about?"

Lilium felt the mud, its weight, and she tried to rest, but the question was more problematic than she anticipated. "Yes."

The shaeman pulled a vase close and began to weave a soothing basket, but did so slowly so that the assassin knew the calming aids would not be given so hastily. "You are haunted, but not by ghosts save for memory."

"Yes," Lilium wanted the mud to crush her as clouds of the past swelled to the surface.

"The paths of a Vanessan Blackroot are troublesome. Not many make it to their trials and few are ever absolved of their guilt."

"I fear not what I have done," Lilium said as she sank deeper into the mud. "Vanessa will take me in bounty to the Fey Wilds. I have earned such rest."

"So sure are we that doors remain open? Guilt is not your weight." The shaeman began to sprinkle a collection of herbs into the bath, but they still refused the to offer the healing basket, "It is the fear of failure."

"I have not failed," Lilium defended herself.

"Yet," the shaeman smiled from the foot of the bath. "You are worried that your calling is too late. You are worried that the deeds you were asked to halt shall go on and you will be moments too late."

"Yes," Lilium admitted.

"You are proud, and you deserve thanks. The assassins of Vanessa are entrusted with sacred tasks beyond the sight of those upon Nhearn. You are called upon by nature itself, tasked with trials that are meant for the betterment of all who reside." The shaeman stood up and bowed to the Blackroot before setting the basket on top of the bath and setting it ablaze with a short whisper. "Thank you for your deeds, past and future. Do not allow doubt to slow you, Lilium of the Blackroot. Your task is at hand. Rest here a moment and think of what it is that Vanessa has asked you to do, for I see that you know not what yet, but that your mind is wrapped in that thought tightly."

As the shaeman left, some of the other elves of Abnogne came to collect what she had left on the ground. Her eyes were sharp as they moved about near her, but despite her concerns the elves did not reach for anything that she had left upon the important bench. The vile dagger remained in its place, wrapped away from any use, and she tried to rest while she was able.

When the servants of Abnogne vacated Terica's room the shaeman entered and sat at the foot of the assassin's bath. "A pair of Blackroot is a dangerous team, not one that is often seen or considered feasible."

"The pleasantries of Abnogne are different today," Terica kept her eyes locked with the shaeman and considered leaving the bath altogether with the suspicious behavior.

"Be still," the shaeman said gently as they began to craft a basket of flowers and herbs in front of her. "There are many who wish to come this day, and each carries with them a wound which needs much attention."

"Mine," Terica asked quietly.

"You are not a Blackroot," the shaeman looked up from their craft and peered into the wood elf's eyes. "Not at heart, though your spirit wishes it was."

"I know this."

"Guilt?"

"Yes," Terica nodded, unable to escape the sight of the shaeman as the mud allowed her to sink only so quickly.

"But this is not your wound today, though it is carried with you always at the forefront of your mind." The shaman set the basket on top of the boiling mud and at the tips of their fingers the woven sprigs began to smolder. "What is your companion contending with?"

"It is the charge of the Blackroot to know," she replied while trying to be kind to the host.

"Or is it that you know not yet what it is you are meant to do?"

Terica allowed her chin to sink into the mud, "I fear that I am not able to help her find what it is I may know from Vanessa."

"She carries a similar burden, but she would not blame you. Why is it that she has brought you with her?"

The smoke of the basket sat on top of the bath pit and eased Terica into comfort as the shaeman stood up to depart the room. "Consider perhaps not what you can offer her, but what it is that you mean to her."

"Thank you for your wisdom, honored one."

Terica rested deeper into the bath and the weight of the mud seemed to be heavier than other times that she had visited Abnogne. The mud crushed all around her, but it was her mind that was squeezed most by the heavy muds and the thoughts of her past rose to the surface as a restless sleep began to take hold. *It was a dark night. Somewhere in a distant room was the sound of her father screaming. He was pleading for them to stop. There was a light as they entered, bright and terrible.* The dream was a blur and then her past swelled again as the memories fought at the crushing mud around her. *It was a dark night. She had been caught by the guard. There were sparks of iron against the metal of her blades. She continued into the room. Before her was a nameless elf who had come from the north to share knowledge which could harm the woodlands if it were shared. There had been a betrayal and this elf had been taken by the enemy instead. They were beaten and tortured already, but she wasn't there to rescue him. From her hand came inevitable death to silence what he had been prepared to share. There were more guards coming into the hall and as she turned to flee there was a bright light.* She woke again with a tremor as she was forced to recall the horrible deeds she had done to others in the name of the Blackroot. *It was a dark night. She made a quick slash, calculated and trained. In her hand she held a dagger of the Blackroot which now dripped with the blood of another pruning. With a single blow she had quelled the human which had been the enemy of Vanessa. She did not know why, but she did not need to know such things. Her god had told her to save them from this menace and she had. The dead body was slumped over the table, scrolls and documents littered the surface and some had shuffled to the floor. The guards had no knowledge that she was in the chambers and the door opened with the sound of what must have been the lady of the house. As she turned the bright light of the hall blinded her vision.* Terica opened her eyes considering the honorable things she delivered to Vanessa for notions of a grander safety. *It was a dark night. There was a bright radiance entering from a hidden portal-*

"Hey," a voice spoke to her in Imperial common, a voice that had no accent of any elven on the tongue. She woke quickly and remained still as her instinct began to drive her actions. *A human,* she knew in a moment, *Midland Imperial, perhaps of nobility or stock from higher rank.* "Hey, are you alright?" Her guard faltered as the confusing tone in the human's voice called out to her. *Concern,* she thought. *What motivation does this human have to lie about pulling my emotions for attention?*

Terica looked about and saw that the mud had been disturbed in her bath, ripples trapped in the viscous clay emanating from her struggles while sleeping. Near her feet was the ash of the shaeman's healing basket that had now been devoured completely by the smoldering embers. The sun had moved westward and the shadows had become long and cool in the late evening hours.

She could hear the human move against the mud of their bath before they asked again, "Are you okay?"

"Fine," she said sharply in common.

"Sorry to bother you," he said politely and sheepishly. "I am new to this place; pardon me if I don't know the custom. I was worried about you, that's all."

Terica of the Blackroot was never sure of kindness and she was already uncomfortable that she had been awoken from her slumber suddenly. She crept out of the mud silently and grabbed her Blackroot blade from the bench. With the practiced art of stealth, she went beneath the canvas curtain away from the sight of the meeting house, hiding low to avoid her shadow against the neighboring pit, and then she crept beneath the colorful curtain into the adjacent room. She was crouched behind the head of the bath and before her was a human.

He had his eyes shut and he seemed to be resting while the ash of the shaeman's basket sank into the mud. The human's items of importance seemed to be ceremoniously placed on the bench, purposefully set down with thought regarding the weight they burdened him with. There was a sword, polished, the sheath well cared for. *Display only*, her experience concluded he would not put up much fight. Her eye fell upon a set of coins that she knew from study. "You are a dragon hunter?"

Basimick opened his eyes and turned around to see the elf crouched over him. He could see that this elf was paler than the others, hidden from the sunlight where she was from, that her demeanor was different, and that the accent was of a different land. Her features were not like those of the shaeman and she had mud upon her as though she were also just a visitor to Abnogne. "I am not sure," he answered. "I suppose that I am, though I have not been one for very long. I don't think that I am, but I have been told that I do well enough for it."

"You have found this place by the grace of your god for your hard work then? Christianna perhaps? The Empire of Man enjoys her praise from what I hear."

"I was led here by an elf, or a spirit of one," he spun his position about to face her properly. "I am lucky; I would not have made it through the grasslands without their help." His heart did not race as he spoke to the stranger, and though his mind wandered to the violent battle of Ovelclutch, he did not assume that she was among the elves there. "I was taken from the grasses and led to this hidden place to rest. Why are you here," he asked, hoping that he wasn't bringing up any upsetting matter that had brought this elf to the mud pits.

"I have been here before. It was shown to me because of my own great accomplishments. It is a place of rest for me and my kin. It rejuvenates us, though I must be dealing with more than usual." As her statement ended she began to realize that she had shared too much with the stranger and she was feeling vulnerable. Terica leaned to return to her bath through the curtain divider between their rooms, but she was halted as he spoke to her.

"I am sorry if I am intruding in this place."

Terica smiled, for perhaps his kind tone was truly without deceit. "All are welcome if they arrive in Abnogne."

As she once again began to leave, Basimick smiled back at her, "Thank you."

The curtain was lifted and she could see that her bath was still holding the form of her disturbances. "If I return then I will have to face those bad dreams again. You asked why I was here."

"Only to be friendly, or to help you if I could. I didn't mean to pry at all."

Terica sat down and with her weapon still hidden from his view she discarded it to her side of the divider. "I thought that I had known what I was doing, but now I am not certain."

Basimick nodded and laughed which seemed to insult her, "No, don't leave, I just. It is the same thing I was thinking about myself."

"What are you supposed to be doing?"

"I was trying to save my village."

"A noble cause," Terica interrupted the rest of his thought.

Basimick frowned and emotion swelled in his chest, "I thought so too."

She couldn't look at him as she faked a laugh, "I suppose such grandeur was something on my mind also."

"It didn't work out that way. I made a terrible mistake." They both took a moment to contemplate on their own thoughts before Basimick spoke again, "And then I was traveling with the dragon hunters to find the dragon again."

"Is that where you go now?" She looked again at the items left around the human's bath. There were three coins of the dragon hunters beside his sword. "Where are the others you were traveling with?"

Basimick sank into the bath and his eyes showed that her words pained him.

Her own gloom became apparent and she continued to look at the items around the bath. There were boots, pants, common clothes, a satchel of dried food and a bladder of water, but as her eyes fell upon the dragon scale jerkin she realized what she had seen in the pyre at the dwarven city. "Were you in Ovelclutch recently?"

Basimick looked at her, unable to speak, and his heart began to grow anxious.

"You were," Terica slouched as the somber realization began to overcome her also.

"Why?"

"Do not be afraid of me, I am no soldier." Terica waited for the human to calm a bit, realizing she must have accidentally threatened him. "I was not at that battle, though I came after it had ended."

"What do you know," Basimick stuttered to ask.

"Your companions, they must have been valiant warriors," she said. She tried to meet his gaze, but she began to feel the ache, and even her own eyes began to swell with the undesired emotions of dark events.

"They are," Basimick smiled for only a moment to thank her for the news. "Were," he stopped to think of how to approach the elf with more questions. He took a deep breath and attempted to smile again, but it wore from his face quickly each time he tried. "Enough about me," he tried to chuckle to transition away from his story. "What about you? What are you supposed to be doing?"

Terica laughed with him as they both tried to make the uneasiness vanish. "I thought I was going to return home, but now I am still traveling."

"Why?"

"I am not done yet with what I was asked to do."

"What were you asked," but his voice trailed away as he thought not to pry so much.

Terica took notice of the human's careful tactic and chose to answer him, "I am not sure. I am usually very sure, but that is not the case this time."

"Is that what was bothering you?"

"Things I have done bother me at times," she studied his face as she uttered her honesty, but he revealed no fear or malicious intent. "This time I am bothered that I have no answer. I was supposed to be helpful, but I fear that I am running out of time to be."

"You are not alone?"

"No, this is something that I also find strange to me."

"Is it hard to be alone?"

Terica thought about the question for a while. "I think that I had liked being by myself when I did not know that I was." They both remained quiet for a time, regaining their strength to continue talking. "Where are you heading now? There is still a distance to travel back to Imperial lands."

"I thought about going to Armontrosia, or Imitheon, or any Imperial city. I need to get help for the dwarf city," he answered.

"Do not do that," she shook her head. "You are brave, and I hate to tell you that Ovelclutch is already beyond help. Sending assistance to that place would be useless now."

"What am I to do instead?" Basimick was beginning to crumble again.

"Get help," Terica smiled at him. "But put that help to use."

"Where?"

"When I passed through that city I was told that the elven army was moving northward and westward. I know that there is an Imperial city there in the woods of Presons. That is where they are going."

"Why would you tell me," Basimick looked her in the eyes. "You don't owe me such a thing."

"I told you, I am not a soldier. I am not sure why we follow them, but perhaps if you were to get help it could assist my companion in some way, and if it does not then I know that I told you and I will help her when such a thing becomes necessary."

"Knowing this might ruin your plan?"

The corner of Terica's mouth showed the curl of a smile. "I told you that I did not know what I was doing. You've ruined nothing."

She began to leave again through her curtain when he said in a genuine and grateful voice, "Thank you."

Terica looked back through the open curtain at him. His eyes were looking at hers, his smile was wide, and he seemed hopeful that something good could be done. "Perhaps, some day, we might meet again."

"I would like that," he said as the curtain fell to separate them from each other.

CHAPTER VIII
ELMINIL MOVES SOUTH

Elminil moved southward again, setting out before dawn as he normally did, and with his rested strength he carried her until the sun came over the eastern peaks. With the first golden rays of sunlight her eyes opened, and as it was every day, she put up a struggle to complain that he had not woken her. "I can carry my own weight," she cried and Elminil let her down gently.

"I know, Abigael, and you do, but you are light yet. I am not troubled by it, and I need less rest than you need to keep your strength high."

She rubbed her eyes and let out a yawn. "How much further south, Mr. White-Waters?"

He laughed, "Not as far as we have come, but a ways longer still." He began looking around and found a pleasant meadow beside the road. "Now that you are awake, let us make a fire and prepare breakfast. We are not in a rush after all." He began unloading some supplies and sent her to gather some fresh wood as he removed the left over tinder from his own traveling packs.

They were both coming out of the far territories north of the Great Sea, passed the dwarven sanctuaries of the coast, and what had once been distant southern regions had become the far north of local cartographies. The coast was rugged, stormy, and full of teeth. To the east were the tall mountains of Dwamaklad, the first wall into the dwarven kingdoms built in the high elevations of Helena's Cradle. It was a narrow passage between the coast and the dwarven range, but Elminil had few other routes to take after their departure from the Northern Territories.

Fog had begun to come in on the wind from the western sea and he sat to make a morning camp before continuing their march for the day. The dancing flames of a simple campfire became hypnotizing and he wore a grim face, as though the crackling of logs were pulling out a great sadness from the depths of antiquity. "Damn elves," he whispered as the smoke turned and stung his eyes.

"You are an elf, Mr. White-Waters."

He was surprised by the noise and more so surprised that he had been startled so simply. Over his shoulder he peered up at the girl who had brought an armful of the driest logs she could find, though they were still damp from the coastal weather. "I am?"

"Yes, Mr. White-Waters."

Elminil laughed at himself and stroked his chin as he fully escaped his trance. "I must have forgotten."

"But you are different, I remember."

"I am glad I have a companion with such a good mind," he reached over and invited her to sit beside him near the fire. "Are you ready?"

"Yes," she said with an infectious smile.

"Good. I would like to continue walking through the next few spans in the daylight and we might have to wait for the fog to clear. I might be able to show you some of the places of old, if they still yet exist in this land." He began to cook some of the rations he had saved as he teasingly asked, "Do you remember how to read?"

Abigael said nothing, but nodded happily.

"Imperial common?"

She nodded.

"Sylvaari?"

She nodded again.

"Nuddish?"

She continued to nod.

"Good, but those will not be much use in these places. These are dwarven lands."

"I can read it," She answered. "I just don't speak dwarven that well, Mr. White-Waters."

"They speak in Imperial common mostly, at least in their outer settlements with all the trade they have going on with the humans. But when we reach the end of our journey south, we will need a whole different dialect entirely."

"Is that why I also know High Elvish?"

Elminil's smile was wide with pride, "That is exactly why. Will you be able to remember what I show you?"

She nodded with excitement of what was to come next.

CHAPTER IX
BASIMICK IN THE PLAINS

Basimick had rested through the night and awoke on a pile of soft hides within the meeting house. There were many rooms that were circling the outer wall, alcoves carved into the chitin and innards of the giant crab. Just like his own space, each room was made for the comfort of visitors, and they each faced toward a center pit where a fire had recently extinguished with use. He looked about the chamber, but discovered that he was alone within the meeting house. He picked up his belongings which had been neatly placed just outside of his alcove. He got dressed and slung the newly packed satchel over his shoulder before tying the scabbard to fasten his sword to his belt properly.

When he exited from the dark of the inner chamber, passing through the central door out of the meeting house, the sun blinded him. As his eyes adjusted the silhouette of the shaeman came into view. "You have come and learned much," they said. "But now you will be tested with these truths upon your journey."

"Thank you for the hospitality," Basimick bowed, trying to capture the pleasantries that the elves had shown to him.

"What do you see us as, young master human?"

"Friends," he said hesitantly, hoping not to be so bold in suggesting such a relationship.

The shaeman smiled, acknowledging a good answer. "And what of the others, for you met another elf too?"

He was not afraid of the elf that had revealed herself, but he was unsure what their meeting had meant. "Friends," he eventually answered.

"Do not fear all over some. This is a simple truth at its core, but it is one that even the elves needed to learn over long years, and perhaps they will need to learn this lesson again." The shaeman smiled and cupped Basimick's shoulder to lead him toward the edge of the clearing. "And do not dwell on what could have been, but master the wisdom shared by what has come to be."

"Honored one," Basimick stopped walking for a moment and they both turned to face one other. "The other elf who visited me, who was she?"

"Remember that Hoopha was a warrior and a chief among his people," the shaeman grinned at Basimick's curiosity. "He was chosen by my lady Katrina, goddess of the winds, and nominated by my ancestors also, to save this land from certain destruction. He spent his life answering the call until so many years had passed that all he knew in his heart was that destruction. This led him to attack the Empire until the border roads were all that was left for them. He saved us, but it left wounds that linger still between us and the humans. For some reason Hoopha saw in you the same path and was drawn back closer to the mortal self that he had once been long ago."

"But she said to me that she wasn't a soldier."

"No, she is perhaps far more dangerous than that, but she is set upon the same path as Hoopha. She is a

Blackroot, an assassin of the Lady of the Fey, of Vanessa, the goddess of nature, and the mother of the elves. Who you met here was a sylvari elf, a wood elf, who was chosen, and perhaps in time she will lose herself to that calling as so many others have before her. She is a servant of a higher calling, much as Hoopha."

"Why would she tell me of the other elves? She told me there is an army of them gathering and where to find them."

"Is that what she did?" The shaeman looked over the grasses and peered as though they could see something stirring in the vacant landscape. "Then perhaps she saw that same destiny within you."

"What is it that you see?"

"I see that you are scared, but I see that you know right from wrong, and that you know good from evil. I see that it pains you to have experienced it in the way that you have, but these scars are lessons for you to use as you travel through your life. When you are called upon for your moment, I think that you will answer the higher calling, as Hoopha in his time, as the wood elf did in hers, and perhaps you can avoid becoming the monster that you fear when it is done."

"Thank you," Basimick bowed his head again as the shaeman led him to the edge of the clearing where tall grass blocked the view forward.

"This direction will take you northward. Guide your path with the sun, east to west as the day, but travel with the stars at night. As you near the end of the horizon you will see the wall of mountains that shall guide you to the border of your Empire." The shaeman then presented Basimick with a necklace. It was a sturdy black thread that had been tooled through the bones of a long finger. "Let it guide you."

He took the horrifying artifact, but he was not afraid. It made him feel safe as he held it and he carefully placed it in the pocket where the three tokens of the dragon hunters resided. "I am so very thankful."

"Do not allow yourself to disappoint Hoopha, young master, nor allow such a fate against yourself."

With a wide gesture the shaeman swung their arm and Basimick took his leave of Abnogne. He crawled through the tall grass and began traveling northward with rejuvenated strength, a full satchel of rations, and his hopes restored. As he escaped the tall fronds, and he was among grasses that he could see over, Basimick turned back, but he could not see the great meeting house any longer. It was hidden among the heights of the golden stalks and he whispered a promise to keep the place secret.

Through the day he stayed at a gentle pace, looking to the sun as it swooped overhead to keep his heading as northward as he could. A cool wind blew through the plains so that all around him were rolling waves of golden grasses, but his eyes no longer strained to discover what was beyond, and he enjoyed the beauty of the world that was now dancing with him.

As night came he was relieved from the baking sun and he traveled more quickly through the grasslands. As he came to the rise of a hill, a wind rolled over him, and he felt an urge to peer westward. From the vantage of the hilltop he could see below the rise where a dried river ditch had opened into a wide dale. The comforting orange glow of large fires illuminated the river basin and the dwellings of the plain elves cast shadows that danced with the flickering flames. There were large structures built to oversee the communal fires, but there was only one blue structure to share for the whole basin. As he stood to see the plain elves in their domain, the wind became calm so that he could hear them singing. He was too far away to make out any words, though he knew he would not understand them if he could. The sound of it through the calm air was mesmerizing and beautiful, but the songs were heavy with a great melancholy.

He smiled, knowing that if he was not meant to witness the elves then he would not have been able to, and he continued to travel north through the starlit night.

CHAPTER X
TOR-TOREK

The two witch hunters pushed forward through the dense forest, cutting their way through vines and underbrush to make their way north toward the sound of the sea striking the cliffs ahead. Evelyn's blade made wide sweeps ahead of her, carving a direct route out of Wilderlands. At last their efforts were rewarded and they broke free of the tree line onto the cliff side road.

"I am surprised that you were able to get us so close to the castle, sister." Alison's silver eyes glared into the dense fog and down the road eastward came a flash of a bright light. "The lord's lighthouse is just ahead."

The two made sure that their armor was presentable, cleaned of any loose vines or mud, and they traveled through the fog toward the western border of the fortress town of Tor-Torek. As they neared their destination, the sound of thundering water guided them toward the first ravine. Below a sharp cliff was the confluence of many streams that met in the Wilderlands and then rushed out into the Crab Bay over the cliffs of the coastline. The only passage was the wide stone bridge that revealed itself with lanterns shining through the morning fog.

The sisters arrived at the border posts of the bridge and a guard revealed himself from the post. He wore decorated heavy steel plated armor and he wielded a shield that was adorned in witch hunter symbols. Over the heart of the breastplate and inscribed on the shield were the insignias of the Tor-Torek witch hunters and above it was the silver moon sigil of Aurora. "Who comes to the lord's keep," the guard called as the pair neared, a common formality to any approaching from Wilderlands.

"You dare question our purpose in our own home," Evelyn shouted, insulted that she had not been recognized.

"Embarrassing," Alison eyed her sister, but she found more disappointment with the guard who had nearly fled from the huntress's tantrum. "Stop your foolishness," and her sister did so. She frowned at the guard but respectfully honored the customary questions of the bridge crossing, "Alison and Evelyn Hnaris, witch hunters of Tor-Torek."

"What is the reason for your return," the guard was hesitant to continue the obligatory conversation.

Alison stared at her sister to ensure cooperation. "We have completed our assignments. We come for respite and new tasks from the master of the keep."

"By the grace of Aurora," the guard bowed to conclude the exchange.

"What was that," Evelyn spat. She looked at Alison, "He adds further insult. Were you not fit to a priestly life in the grace of Christianna, bridge watcher?"

The guard bowed their head and uttered a quick apology, though he was unsure of what had been done. "She is right," Alison stated coldly, her silver eyes shining through the fog at him. "If I were more worried that you were capable of accomplishing anything then I would consider you to be false. For now I will consider you to merely be ignorant and new."

"What did I-"

"Walk in moonlight," Alison said as she walked passed him.

Evelyn waited for Alison to take a few paces on the bridge before she began to cross it herself. "Remember me, neophyte. I will not be halted at the threshold of my own home again." Evelyn leaned over the guard as she passed and he hid himself from her presence. "Walk in moonlight."

Evelyn caught up to her sister who was politely bowing her head to all the new guards that were stationed along the bridge. "There are many new faces here, Evelyn."

"I smell fear on them."

They were welcomed onto the witch hunter grounds by the guards as they stepped off of the bridge but they offered nothing more than a nod to the new recruits. The sisters continued through the fog toward the light that flashed over the silhouettes of the buildings that surrounded the keep ahead. Alison began to offer a brief wave of the hand to the people alongside the path. They were dressed in simple robes and bowed their heads to the huntresses as they continued to tend to the bountiful fields that grew between the western and eastern ravines. "Acknowledge them sister," she instructed. "They are owed at least that respect."

"Injured hunting the witches, retired from the hunt, left to tend to the castle," Evelyn began to wave as the farmers appeared from out of the fog. "Do not let me waste away to such a fate."

"Aurora would not allow such an ending for either of us," Alison agreed.

At last they arrived at the outer wall of the township proper, but they became disappointed at the imposing obstacle before them. There was a lot of noise and commotion throughout the town as the merchant caravans from the city of Tronia arrived alongside a wandering pilgrimage from the churches of Southrunn. The streets were crowded as veteran witch hunters looked for deals among the carriage stalls and old members of Tor-Torek lined groups of young clerics along the walls to keep eyes out for fresh recruits. They both entered the street with a plain look of disdain for the chaos, but many in the street moved aside as they realized who was crossing their path.

As they traversed the center plaza of town they encountered a large crowd of robed church clerics who were attempting to look strong as an older hunter inspected them. Many called out to get his attention, making claims that they could end the witch scourge themselves or rival the best that Tor-Torek had to offer, but it did not draw out a response from the recruiter. His attention drifted away from the crowd and he shouted, "Huntresses, just in time. Come here for a moment and help me with this rabble."

Evelyn smiled, hoping that the recruiter might actually allow for the clerics to make good on their threats of fighting the best, but Alison revealed nothing as she turned toward the crowd.

The old recruiter studied the youths before him and plucked one from the crowd. As he did the Christiannan priest who was accompanying the pilgrims began to request that another might be taken, yet the recruiter paid no mind to their pleas. "Huntresses, in your wisdom, what do you see in this one?"

Alison stood beside the old man and peered at the youth through her silver lit eyes, "I see innocence in this one. He has not yet been challenged."

Evelyn stood to the other side of the recruiter, shook her head with disappointment that the others with more bravado were not being checked, and gazed upon the youth with her own piercing silver eyes, "No sister, it is weakness. He must have avoided such tests."

The youth was afraid of the hunters, but he managed to shake the grip of the recruiter and told Evelyn, "I am of kind heart, I wish no harm, but I am not weak."

"Incapable," Evelyn corrected herself.

"Not every task requires violence, but knowing to commit to action when necessary is important." Alison inspected the youth more closely, nearly as interested in him as the recruiter was. "What would you do for the greater good?"

"Aurora's will," he answered.

Alison looked at the priest who was hiding from her eyes, aware perhaps of what it meant to look at her, then her gaze met the recruiter, "Is this one to be chosen for the true trials?"

"None of these other ones would survive that feat," the recruiter answered. "You know what it takes, moon gifted. What do you think of this one?"

Alison's silver gaze fell back onto the youth and lingered there for a moment. "Allow this one onto the boat," she said at last. "Use my authority for his passage."

"Do not disappoint her," Evelyn glared at the youth who was still staring at her.

The recruiter grabbed the boy by the shoulders before any further conversation could be had among them, "You are a good lad. I can feel good things from you to come." The crowd became irate, but as Evelyn smiled the priest quickly instructed them to disband and find other recruiters. Alison paid no more attention to the matter and continued toward the lighthouse tower. Evelyn followed behind her sister, but as she passed one of the more bold youths who had ignored the priest's instruction, she postured to scare him and he fell to his knees before her in fear.

The sisters passed through the rest of town and neared the gate into the keep's courtyard. Two guards, each adorned in the fine armor of the witch hunters of Tor-Torek, nodded and stepped aside to allow them entry without a word shared among them. As they crossed the threshold the noise of the street disappeared. They moved through the courtyard garden, not once bothering to take a moment to notice the exotic or delicate things kept there, nor did they offer any amusement or care to the statuary or fountains in the massive collection. Instead they went straight to the door of the castle's keep at the foundation of the lighthouse tower and entered.

Inside was dimly lit as only a few of the available sconces were lighting the incredible collection gathered throughout the castle. Trophies, weapons, armors, books, artifacts, and curiosities of a well-traveled gatherer were on display in the halls and within the rooms of the gloomy place. The sisters did not bother with it, distractions were all they were to them and they had business only with the master of the keep. They moved through the dark halls to the furthest chamber from the entry door and entered into a room that was brightly lit by daylight coming through the tall narrow windows overlooking the bay. All around the walls were shelves of books and atop each table were more massive tomes that had been opened to be studied.

"Lord Calcifor," they both said as they closed the door behind them. They maneuvered around the pedestal at the center of the room, and neared the window where the lord of the keep sat in a fine chair looking out toward the sea.

"There are only a few new recruits on that boat this day," he stood up and offered the view from the window. "We used to send dozens."

"Weakness lingers on these new ones," Evelyn answered. "The guards posted at the bridge's reek of fear. I imagine most of these new recruits today will not survive Aurora's trials when they arrive at the sanctuaries."

"Even that one," Calcifor pointed to the boat leaving the shore. "I am sure that he is looking at this very window."

Alison was still, staring down at the rocky coastline below where the crews manning the departing ships fought against the crashing waves of the Crab Bay. "I have faith in that one, but it is beyond our grasp now. We shall see what they may accomplish in time."

"Yes, indeed," The man nodded and he glanced at the artifact in the center of the room briefly. "How were your assignments?"

"The witch near Seven Bridges was taken care of quickly." Evelyn tried to recollect how long their journey had been this time, "And the fire starter was easy to find."

Calcifor smiled at the news, "I am glad to hear your successes. The other witch hunters I have since sent have had a difficult time discovering who has the blight apart from citizens. They seem to have to wait until the witch reveals themselves, which is never good." He looked to Alison, "What of the noble girl, the one with the cancerous effects."

"I fear there may still be lingering effects in the Wilderlands," Alison stated. "The potency of that final witch, along with the lengthy period of their manifestation, could have allowed for migrations of the afflicted."

"There were giant creatures," Evelyn clarified.

Calcifor waved off the idea of loose ends, "So long as the source is gone we have done good work by Aurora. Nhearn will always have heroes willing to find such foes as large lizards or strange bugs. Give it time and we may yet hear of such tall tales, but truly the greater good has been done and we should appreciate that the source of these creatures has ended."

"What of our next assignments," Evelyn asked with zeal.

"This next task draws you away to the north." He went to the center of the room and thought to lift the cover from the pedestal but held himself from the temptation. "I received news that our church across the bay has fallen from our noble path."

"Infighting," Evelyn smiled, for she was eager for a true test of her skill.

Alison ignored the excitement, "Why condemn their sect? If I am not mistaken, that sanctuary is a collective of shrine tenders. They shouldn't have any responsibilities other than cleaning the moon shrines along the road there."

Calcifor was quiet for a moment and then turned away from the pedestal toward a desk where he began inscribing notes into one of the many open tomes. "There is a rumor that they are harboring enemies and witches within the sanctuary itself. There is an epidemic in Bogramville. The city is afflicted with the blight, but the church does not see what it has done. They have been hiding their true purpose and the citizens are becoming restless."

Alison nodded, "Then it shall be done. What shall we attend to after?"

The lord of the keep sat at the desk but his mind thought again to unveil the pedestal and seek answers. He hesitated and looked at the sisters, "I am unsure of what has yet to transpire, the mysteries of the future have darkened my spirit, and I trust no others with the noble responsibility of good deeds. There will be a moment, I am sure of this, and when the time comes for you to witness that time I am sure that you will have the guidance of Aurora with you."

Alison's silver eyes glared at the pedestal with intrigue. "You speak as though you were a prophet, Calcifor."

He stood up from his seat and placed the book which had no title into a place among the many shelves. "Travel north from the sanctuary in Bogramville with your own wits. See to our church in Tronia that they might be untainted, and from there take which ever path seems fitting to you. Take what risk may come and when Aurora calls you home you may return. You are Aurorans. You will know what is best for Nhearn when you are asked to judge."

"You intend for us to adventure," Evelyn asked.

Calcifor leaned into his chair and closed the book he had been writing in. "I intend for you to find your own purpose now."

CHAPTER XI
BASIMICK DISCOVERED

The Great Plains had been like an endless sea, the grass rolling with the breeze like golden waves out to the horizon. The only direction that he could discern was by the rising and setting sun so that at each twilight he would wade into the grasslands northward as best he could tell beneath the stars. He was warned that the journey through the Great Plains would still test him, but with blessings of the shaeman and of Hoopha, he knew there would be little danger from the people of the grasslands or the animals hiding in the landscape. He trekked through the tall grasses northward alone, for none of the other guests to the sacred baths of Abnogne had left with another, nor had they seemed to travel in the same direction.

Without anyone else to speak with, his mind wandered to the other visitors and who they must have been. *Who was the assassin that aided me during my stay, or the companion that she had arrived with? Who was Tydas and why did the shaeman speak so highly of him?* These were more comforting distractions than the thoughts that he had been dwelling on when he entered the plain lands from Ovelclutch, but even those terrible feelings encroached often.

As dawn began to show on the eastern horizon of the third day he could at last see the landmark on the edge of the world as the shaeman had claimed. It was far away still, days of walking yet to go, but the distant silhouette of the peaks were now in view to give him direction and hope. The Cragged Mountains, the wall of stone, now guided him, the bleak and lifeless rock of legend showing the way back toward the borders of the Empire. As he got closer, the mountains quickly became larger, the great cliffs rising into the clouds and beyond. Some peaks were so sharp that they appeared as claws and teeth, gnashing into the clouds as heavy mists were swept through the narrow gorges between the mountains by the western winds. At the great summits were white caps of snow that cast storm clouds into the sky as the sun struck the faces of the mountains. As the days continued, the sights ahead of him were only the gray rock of the mountains which stood high above the horizon so that they dominated as far to the east and as far to the west as his sight could allow.

Basimick traveled for many more days through the waving grass, crossing over the occasional dry creek bed, and at times he was lucky enough to witness the wildlife revealing itself before it vanished again forever. As he neared the base of the mountains he began to risk travel throughout the day, the sight of them spurring him on, and during the late evening of the eleventh day, Basimick reached the road at last.

It was a wide path, rutted slightly by cart and carriage, and it was barren of grass. As he stepped into the road he looked eastward. The road curved around hills so that it remained without incline, it was clear of any unpleasant obstacles, and it was comfortable underfoot. To the south of the road was a clear border of tall grass that began the lands of the Great Plains.

With surprise, Basimick was happy to see that none of the grassland south of the road was touched by the Imperials who cared and tended for the road itself. To the north Basimick could see a woodland that was green and thick with vegetation that grew from the distant waterfalls which fell from the cliffs of the Cragged Mountains.

He turned west and he could see that the Cragged Mountains curved southward, an arm of the range reaching out many spans away from where he was, but it revealed no city or Imperial holds. He turned back to the east and wondered which direction he needed to head to find help. He sat into the grass on the southern edge of the road and opened his satchel. There were some rations left, but the many days of travel had taken its toll on his supplies. Tired of traveling through the day under the sun, and unsure of the distance to any Imperial city, he laid down to close his eyes to wait for daybreak.

"Wake up," a jab into the ribs did just that and Basimick woke with a sudden fright. "Woah there, I'm friendly. Be happy I wasn't an orc or grass elf though. They would not be so kind if they had found you sitting on their side of the border here."

Basimick sat up and was more surprised to find faces his own age than he was to discover it was already early morning. He rubbed his eyes to remove the blur of waking, though he was dizzy with sleep and his body ached with fatigue from crossing over the plains.

"I didn't mean to hurt you if I did. You weren't waking up to shouts and I even rolled you over a bit. You didn't seem too well off and I needed to wake you if I could."

Basimick's eyes at last adjusted and he could see the *friend.* He was about the same height, but much more slender in the shoulders. The stranger wore a loose fitted white shirt that was cinched by a belt, in which was strapped a dagger, just above the waist.

"My name is Lin," he said, arm outstretched to greet Basimick who sat up and gathered his belongings from the grass.

"I am Basimick of Kurrum," he returned the pleasantries and took Lin's outstretched arm. He was heaved up quickly and he caught himself on the tips of his toes before he stumbled forward.

There were many others gathered about him, all young, each dressed in the same simple shirt and pants that were all so wildly fitted they must have been clothes of charity, not tailored. Along the road were several carriages in a line pulled by a variety of oxen from across the territories of Nhearn. "Pleasure to have met you, Basimick of Kurrum," Lin shook his hand and at last let go, only now being confident in Basimick's ability to stand. "We here are members of the Red Circus, a traveling act of sorts." Lin looked around and thought to introduce the others, but so many had gathered around them that he chose not to overwhelm the newcomer.

Basimick attempted to dust himself off, though the many days' worth of travel had become stuck deep into the cloth of his tunic. He adjusted his sword into a presentable position and tried to see everyone he could in the eyes. "A pleasure to meet you all," he said. "More so now than ever. I was lost in the plains for some time and I could use some help with direction on the road."

Lin laughed in a way that long friends would, "Then truly you are lucky we are not orc or elves, truly."

Basimick nodded and sighed with relief, "Very lucky." Lin's laugh reminded Basimick of Marccus and he became comforted in that thought. "Very lucky indeed."

Lin smiled, "Where are you heading? Never a pleasant thing to travel alone."

Basimick looked into the tall waving grasses that seemed flat and endless all the way to the horizon in the south. He took a deep breath in and let it out so that he could relax a bit more in his shoulders. "Never alone, those are words of wisdom," he smiled at Lin who was still nodding and laughing. "I want to go to a city, Lin, but I admit I do not know the way there."

"You are in luck yet again, my friend," Lin pointed west. "We are going now to the great city of Imitheon. It is not much farther from where we are and for you not much farther than where you've come."

An elf girl stepped forward from the ring of onlookers, "You cannot invite people into the caravan, Lin. You must get permission from Ulric."

Lin's smile faded for only a moment and it did not seem that the elf noticed the discomfort. His smile returned and he pointed to another member of the Red Circus who had gathered in the crowd. "Wake him, Hilde, if you don't mind. We would not want to leave our new friends behind would we?"

Basimick smiled, a bit uncomfortable that he may have been thrust into a potential squabble, but his composure remained friendly, just as his father had taught him during guard duty in Kurrum. The girl turned around and jabbed a finger into another youth whose shirt jingled with a collection of hidden metals, "Go get Ulric, love." The clinking within his shirt worsened as he sped off toward the rear of the carriage line.

"I'm sure it will be fine," Lin whispered. "Ulric is a very agreeable man."

The morning light was cast from behind the man and Basimick strained to see into the silhouette as he approached. He was older, much taller than the others, and he wore fanciful robes that were most certainly tailored and paid for, not donated. The crowd of youths separated to let the man through and Lin made an awkward overly performed bow as the man neared them. "Haurus tells me that Lin has found yet another distraction for us." Some of the others laughed, but the man kept a very regal tone. He looked at Basimick who now felt a bit underdressed to meet the leader of this troupe. "A dragon hunter? Very well. You have outdone yourself this time, Lin."

"I am no dragon hunter, sir," Basimick was quick to say. "I suppose I could have been though."

"What are you doing out this way then?"

Basimick chuckled a bit and Ulric leaned in, now curious for the answer. "I had been hunting a dragon, sir."

"A strange coincidence it seems," Ulric smiled at the discovered irony. "You will have to tell me your tale of how you got the costume of an Imperial dragon hunter and chose to chase down a dragon while on unofficial business." Everyone laughed as did Basimick who was becoming more comfortable with everyone around him. "Come then," Ulric waved to Basimick as he turned to go back to his personal carriage. "Join us on our merry way. No one should be left alone to fend off the dangers of the Trade Road." He took a few steps and Basimick began to follow, but suddenly the man turned about with his hand outstretched, "Ulric Reddon, at your service, master hunter."

"Basimick, son of Bassar," he wanted to sound more respectful to a man who owned a last name.

"Bassar of Havvel?"

Basimick smiled wide, "That's the one!"

"The Lord's servant. That man managed to arrest me more times than any other in all the Empire."

Basimick's smile vanished, "Oh, I-"

Ulric laughed his true laugh, "As he should have. Always the gentleman he was. Be happy your father was a respectable man, as much so as I was surely not." Ulric continued to chuckle to himself as he waved everyone back to their morning duties. "Strange how small Nhearn is with how long it takes to get anywhere."

CHAPTER XII
BASIMICK AND THE
RED CIRCUS

The caravan had been traveling the whole day and after dusk the train of carriages halted for the night in a clearing on the north side of the road. They made camp against the dense woodlands that grew from the springs of the Cragged Mountains, the overgrown forest denying any such waters to the grasslands, which the Red Circus members had warned Basimick that he might have been cursed with bad luck for his trespass over the border of the Trade Road. To the west was the shadow of the mountains stretching southward and the road curved far to the south to avoid any incline over the range. As darkness came and the members of the circus settled into the encampment for the night, several fires were made alongside the caravan.

Basimick found one where more familiar faces had gathered and he sat on a log that must have been dragged over from the woods, though Basimick could not see any trail from where it had come. Lin sat down next to the dragon hunter and handed him a ceramic mug filled with a dark drink. "Not much farther and we will be in the Imitheon Valley. It's a vast flatland of winding roads between the arms of the Cragged Mountains. The whole place has an Age's worth of signposts littering the whole valley from crisscrossing trade routes and shortcuts as far as you can see."

"All the way to southern side where Black Range sit," Mebruk added, sipping from an enormous tin of his own dark drink.

They were gathered around the large fire, the youth of the Red Circus and Basimick enjoying each other's company as the caravan hauling animals rested through the night and grazed in the north side meadow. Lin blew on his drink which was steaming, "Montontra makes the whole thing ominous I suppose."

"I have heard of this place," Kalara said as she refused the opportunity of a dark drink of her own and Haurus took the spare drink to Hilde where he sat. "I've seen the borders of the Forbidden Lands, but that place is not on fire."

Mebruk who sat beside the elf scratched his chin, "What is this, eh, Forbidden Land?"

"Elves call it that," Kalara looked up at the enormous man. "I think you humans call it the Badlands."

"Dwarves call it Badlands too," Lin added as he leaned into the fire so that the glow cast sinister shadows from under his chin. "Montontra is different from the eastern lands though. It is a dark and unforgiving place, ruled only by the orc. They say that nothing lives there except the orc, and they eat their own kind to stay alive. Rivers of lava are the only light and the smoke from the volcano has blocked out the sunlight since prehistory. No man, or elf, or dwarf, or anything other than the orc of the Fire Clans, have ever seen beyond the Mouth of Montontra."

Basimick took a sip of the dark drink and found it terribly bitter, but the warmth of it felt good against the chill that came from the gusts down the slopes of the frigid high mountains. "That's not true."

"You have been called out for your tall tales, Lin," Haurus laughed.

"Your new friend might take your place as the fireside storyteller," Hilde continued to jest with Haurus.

Lin ignored the comments as the others joined together in laughter, "And you have seen inside the lands of fire, Basimick? Do tell."

"I've not been there, but you said that nothing else lives in Montontra, but that is not true, for inside that terrible place is another, and not just in any random place either." Basimick had their attention and all who were gathered around the fire leaned in close to listen.

"Who," Lin asked. "Where?"

"In the great volcano itself. In the cauldron of Mhat-Ozogra, the greatest of all dragons lives," and the audience gasped at his claim.

"You, hunter, are you going into den of monsters," Mebruk waited for the hunter to answer with an intense stare.

Basimick realized that he had shared more than he wanted to, "Someday, perhaps."

The large muscular man raised his drink to honor the hunter. "Luck and gods be with you."

"There is a dragon in the south of Twin Rivers," Kalara said. "They say it has ripped the land so much that nothing will grow. You will go to fight such a thing, in a volcano no less?"

"Bravery," Haurus said and he raised his cup to the hunter. "Luck and gods be with you."

"Foolishness I think," Hilde commented. "But I am not the professional." She raised her cup, "Luck and gods be with you."

Lin stoked the fire before getting comfortable beside Basimick once more. He noticed that his new friend had retreated from the audience and he struck his cup to get everyone's attention away from Basimick. "Perhaps another story, something not so close to our heading. I'd hate to meet the dragon for calling it by name around the fire."

The Red Circus group collected small pebbles from the dirt and flung them at Lin. "Inviting bad magic," they all shouted as Basimick hid from the pelting.

"You know better than that, Lin," Haurus chuckled.

With a laugh and a wave of the hand, Lin comforted Basimick that he was not hurt. "What about the *Escape from Trovania*?"

"Old tale," Mebruk gurgled through a long gulp of his dark drink. "Something this Age."

"I recently escaped from somewhere, if that is a story you want to hear," Basimick offered.

"No need to feel like you have to share," Lin offered.

"Come now, we are all bored of the old stories," Mebruk smiled wide.

Basimick did feel excited to have a crowd around him again, and for a moment he wasn't thinking of the grief returning. "There was a battle, and a sewer."

The youth were all entertained with his story, although there were details omitted and his emotions forced him to dodge details that were not necessary to the ending. He told them about the noise of a thousand arrows striking metal rooftops, and the worry of traveling unseen through the streets of a whole city. He claimed to have found a sewer entrance for he knew the details of a magical woman would lead to questions that he could not answer in his own telling. He spoke of the smell, but that he carried on to save his own life, and the story ended with him entering the grasslands, for he did not want to scare them with ghost stories of the grasses across the road, and he did not want to betray any trust he had with the mud pit oasis.

"Sewers," Lin laughed. "Elves don't use sewers?"

Kalara folded her arms as the question eventually found its way to her, "You would carve a hole through the heart roots of your home and send that to fester in the wood?"

"Where does it go?"

Hilde stopped the question, "The fire pit is a sacred place, Lin."

"But you do know of sewers," Lin asked against Hilde's request, though everyone was intrigued by the elf's answer.

She was hesitant for a moment, looking around at all the other members of the circus before finally giving an answer to the curious lot. "Yes, we know of them. I'm sure it is just an old wives tale that we don't, or it could be a rumor made up by dwarves to make us look weird to you all."

"Well, not having sewers isn't too weird," Lin got the attention back and tried to offer Kalara some respite from the group. "It's no different than an Imperial noble. They get the servants to do the dirty work."

Haurus shrugged at the notion, "The Empire has sewers, Lin."

"Not in the keeps or in the palaces they don't. The residents up at the top are worried about assassins in the pipes. Not since the First Age when Amnith had an issue with that Annabellan demon."

Mebruk set his cup down harshly, "I do not like that story, Lin. Is disgusting!"

"We just listened to a story about a man who crawled out of a sewer." Lin was pelted by another round of pebbles for which Basimick joined into the ritual. "Perhaps if I brewed more bitter water you'd all forgive me," and the crowd of them, even Basimick who had slowly come to enjoy the taste of the dark drink, allowed forgiveness as Lin went to prepare another round of the bitter water for the night.

CHAPTER XIII
AGNITHIA
TAKING ARGENKUL

The elves moved south along the Marching Road through the flat lands that had filled with smoke from the dead city of Ovelclutch. Agnithia and the forces of the Sentinel Woods, combined with the few warriors of the Twin River grove lands that the queen had allowed, used the thick cover of death to reach the foothills of the dwarven held range along the southern coast of the Inland Sea. In the red haze of evening the army could see the glint of the metal spires at the summits of the mountains.

"Why have we taken the south road," one of the lords from the Twin Rivers asked of the general. "The White Queen has moved north into the Great Plains."

Agnithia made a long frustrated hiss before answering, "There are dwarves still among these mountains. The queen was clear that none shall remain upon the face of this world or hide in the depths of the earth."

The elf of high stratum boldly stated, "This battle will be costly."

"What makes you say such things," one of the dark robed lieutenants spoke for the general.

"Argenkul will have seen the smoke of the city. They will know that danger is coming, even if there were no messengers to say so. We are traveling with a column of soldiers along a road that they watch. Even if there were only a score of soldiers left in those peaks they would have the advantage of the high ground, their fortress, and their preparations."

The dark moon shaeman had not left the side of the general since their departure from Ovelclutch and they turned to look directly at the speaker from the Twin Rivers. "You worry that the Fey Mother will not be able to protect you when we challenge the Earth. There is no need to deny your worry. You have not left your lands before, and the Fey Wilde is still near to your heart, but the protections of Vanessa have coddled you."

The lord was upset, but they remained silent as the others from the Sentinel Woods already seemed aware of a plan that had not been shared among their allies.

"Get the camps readied," Agnithia demanded of the Twin Rivers lord. "Light as many torches as we need and then double it. Each band should make a fire to rest for the night."

"Will we attack at daybreak?"

Agnithia held a closed fist up and silenced the lord, "The Twin Rivers will do as they are asked."

As the army arrived at the crossroad where an eastern trek led toward the slopes of the mountain range, they began to make their camps. The elves of the Sentinel Woods warned the Twin Rivers elves to avoid the open fields and light as many flames as they were able in the encampment beside the road. The sun fell beyond the mountain of Aboraeve and in the dim the elven force appeared to be a massive army beside the Imperial roadway.

"There is no moon tonight," the dark shaeman breathed in the night air. "The timing of this effort is divinely gifted to us."

"Then we shall begin," Agnithia uttered. At the general's order, the lieutenants dispersed and gathered all the warriors of the Sentinel Woods.

The sky was dark and the whole army approached the slope of Argenkul beneath the shadow of night. Agnithia was first to step upon the stone where the dwarves took over care of the roads from the Empire of Man. It was built from massive brick placed along the ridge of the mountain, carved smooth with a pleasant grade, and at even intervals were towers beside the road to guard the passage up to the fortress at the summit above. The dark shaeman and the servants around them chanted in a quiet tone to protect the stealth of the whole army. The elven host filled the wide road and began up the slope.

With a wave of her hand, Agnithia sent several dark clad warriors to the first set of towers. They were able to travel ahead of the elven forces, enter into the towers, dispatch the dwarves within, and capture the road checkpoint before any signal was made. They left the blaze of the tower braziers lit so that the guard tower still appeared occupied and as they looked down the slope into the flatland they could see the massive army encamped below. It seemed like a large force had been using the Marching Road and had settled beside it for the night, the fires inviting for march weary soldiers to rest until dawn, much the same as the Imperial armies had done when they stayed on the road near the Sentinel Woods.

The process was made again, capturing the next set of towers under the cover of darkness, the encampment remaining beside the road without alarm, the towers remaining lit without concern, and Agnithia's forces approached the peaks without effort. Just passed the mid of night, Agnithia stepped into the light of Argenkul's main gate. As she stepped forward, the few guards for the night looked down from the wall and could only see the general.

"Why come you at this foul hour? No warning for your comin' either. Do you come rude or with bad tidings, visitor."

Agnithia looked up at them and the dwarves coward slightly as the general's mask revealed itself, the metal reflecting under the flaming lamps beside the gate.

"Not an Imperial man if ever I seen one. Whose army sits at the road?"

She still gave no answers, but instead she raised her hand and pointed at the guards. Her hand moved about and the dwarves above became uncomfortable as she pointed at each and every one of the guards along the western gate wall.

"What is it then? What business are you bringin' with you?"

From the dark beyond the lamp lights came deadly strikes. The clattering armor along the ramparts pulled the dwarves' attention away from the visitor and they realized that arrows had stricken several guards down. Before a signal was raised more arrows struck the dwarves and all the guards along the tower were felled quickly.

The dark shaeman remained at the edge of the light, "The dark moon has kept our secret. Before the guard changes we must press the advantage."

Agnithia waved and the dark clad elves rushed into the light to find paths along the bricks of the wall so they could climb up onto the ramparts. Within moments the gate was opened, weights and chains wildly moving the mechanisms to lower the stone door into the carven pit beneath the threshold so that the army could pass through into the city of Argenkul.

CHAPTER XIV
BASIMICK AND ULRIC

Lin opened his arms and enjoyed the sunlight on his shoulders for a moment, smiling as he listened to Basimick who had become comfortable enough to tell the full tale of his travels. "You blame yourself too harshly, friend."

Basimick tried to capture the rays of enjoyment as Lin did, but the story of his adventure told all at once had been tiresome and painful. "I don't know how I could see it any other way."

"Your hunter companions, the wills bless them where they be, they would have attacked the dragon when they came across it. As you told me, they knew exactly where the dragon was-"

"Yes."

"-and when they had found it, what action would you think they had taken?"

"I suppose you are right."

Lin's smile wavered and he put a hand on Basimick's shoulder. "You might not have even known of the danger in the mountains near your village should it have happened anyway."

Basimick nodded.

"They were heroes at the battle though," Lin tried to make his friend feel better about their assumed fate. "They took up arms, guarded the gate for the refugees, took charge of the battle before them, and I would guess that they knew you could get out of the city when they told you to leave. You did after all!"

Basimick continued to nod.

"They saw that in you and now you get to be the hero they knew you were going to be."

"I don't feel like a hero."

"You, Basimick of Kurrum, dragon hunter of the Empire, acting captain of the guard of that Empire, are choosing to seek out a dragon and at the same time rescue people you don't know from a war that no one else knows about." Lin pulled Basimick close, "I think you are a good hero. I am glad we met. I will get to say to others that I knew that man. I rescued that man!"

The road began to turn southward as it neared the arm of the Cragged Mountains, and as the caravan continued along the Trade Road, Kalara revealed herself to the pair. "Lin. Ulric has requested the company of the dragon hunter to his personal cabin."

"Oh," Lin's smile disappeared. "Well then, we wouldn't want to keep him waiting for his guest."

Basimick noticed the sudden change, "What is it, Lin?"

There was a moment of hesitation, "I just really enjoyed the company. Not too often we meet someone new that I would wish as much good luck upon."

"Come now, hunter." Kalara shook her head toward the rear of the caravan and began to lead him toward Reddon's carriage.

"Thank you, Lin. I didn't think I would enjoy telling anyone what had happened."

"I am happy to have been of some service to you," and with a bow Lin's smile returned to his face as they parted ways for the moment.

After marching against the direction of the caravan they arrived at the rear carts where Kalara knocked upon the door of the grand looking personal carriage of Ulric Reddon. While the two oxen still pulled the wheels forward the door swung open and Ulric held out his hand to pluck Basimick from the road. "Thank you, Kalara."

"Anything else, Master Reddon," she asked while keeping pace with the open door.

"I am sure I will come up with more tasks soon. Feel free to spend your time nearby."

"Of course," she said sweetly and as she stopped to bow the carriage left her behind so that she fell out of Basimick's view.

Ulric closed the carriage door and all of the noise of the traveling circus vanished. To either side of Basimick were comfortable benches, one wide enough to sleep upon, and there were luxurious items packed away on shelves and beneath the seats. "Welcome in once again," Ulric smiled wide and sat himself into the many pillows that were gathered so that he could lounge. "I am sorry to have called you in while we were still moving, though it is hard to slow the caravan from the rear as it were."

"No issue, sir."

"Come now, we have no need for formality like this. I may be blessed with a surname, but it hardly compares to the title of an Imperial dragon hunter. If anything I should be yielding to you, Master Basimick."

Basimick sat across from Ulric and got comfortable on the fine cushions. "If you don't mind, why is it that I was summoned?"

"We are nearing the first gate into Imitheon. There are many dangers ahead and there are several fortifications that keep watch for the city. Never has the city been assaulted in all its time and we have the watchful eyes of the Imperial Legion to thank for it, but it also means that we pay our fair share in toll when the road crosses their path."

"Would I pay more?"

"No," Ulric replied immediately. "And with vestments like yours you will never pay a toll again in your life."

"Perhaps I could-"

"No," Ulric interrupted the offer. He smiled even wider, "That time will come."

"Then why am I here?"

"You had told me when we first met that you needed to get to the city, and I am a man of my word in taking you there. If the soldiers were to witness you coming, I would imagine that they might have pressing business with you, one way or another." Ulric leaned forward and rested on his knees. "The toll for the caravan at this checkpoint is little compared to a bit of assistance at the gate of the city."

"Of course," Basimick's discomfort began to wane as Ulric relaxed. "Thank you for considering me."

"Absolutely. I wouldn't want you to be bogged down in Imperial semantics when you have tasked yourself with good purpose now."

As they spoke together the caravan began to turn sharply alongside the final slopes of the eastern arm of the Cragged Mountains and the driver of their carriage knocked upon the roof. Ulric knocked back to signal the driver to continue and they both peered out of the window to see what was ahead.

Before them was an Imperial fortress manned by soldiers of the Legion. The walls were built of quarried stone from the mountain and constructed to use the carved cliff side of the southern tip of the eastern arm of the Cragged Mountains as its northern defense. The fortress keep was tall enough that it could be seen from the road and it was built against the cliff at the north end of the fortification to look out over the widening mouth of the valley ahead. The walls defended a massive yard and stretched out southward to lie across the road so that any who were traveling east or west around the sheer mountains must pass through their gates or risk trespassing in the grasslands. "Welcome to the eastern fortress of Felceon, master hunter. The eyes here keep the city of Imitheon safe from the tyranny of anything that would come from the east and I have heard they keep their sights also on the orc lands just south of the valley ahead."

As the head of the caravan arrived at the gate the guards atop the wall began to shout and several more guardsmen pushed the gate of the fort open. Basimick watched through the window as the caravan moved under the gatehouse, the height of it just tall enough to allow for Ulric's carriage to pass under, so long as the driver ducked.

Basimick looked around, took in the simple place, focusing then on the wall that was made of bleak gray stone that matched the mining scars from the cliff side. The height of the wall where the soldiers patrolled was only as tall as the wooden palisade of Kurrum, and he frowned at it.

Ulric noticed the youth's disappointment, "Not impressed, young master?"

"I am worried."

"Are the walls here too high for you?"

"Not high enough. How is this place defensible? Why even call it a fortress? I can see the tower there, but it will not last long."

"Not much would last against a dragon. Even the Imperial capital of Amnith itself would tremble before the wake of mighty Olag."

Basimick shook his head, "The elves are coming this way. A whole army of them. The arrows would have no trouble with these walls and the elves would raze this place to the ground without even needing a thought of strategy for it."

"Your worry is misplaced," Ulric told Basimick. "If your tales with me have revealed anything it is that these elves are heading to dwarven territories. They would not need to involve themselves with Felceon, or with Imitheon for that matter."

"But the Empire has dealings with dwarves, right? Even in my village there were dwarves. Would they not attack here?"

Ulric looked at the sight of the fortress before leaning back into his comfortable seat. "This isn't where the elves would come. Look passed the wall, master hunter, do not be blind to the true purpose of this place."

Basimick looked at the yard contained within the walls. The fortress keep was at the north end and was not an impressive sight. The caravan moved along the road at the south end of the yard where at the east and west were gates that guided the road as it passed through the walls. Between the road and the keep however, were hundreds of people wandering about an intricate network of rutted paths and pitted rings. Ruined tents and old pavilions were littered about in no discernable order. There were crowds around bonfires, merchant stalls attempting to peddle out food, all about were large buckets where people filled cups for water, and everywhere was filth. "Why do these people live this way, in squalor?"

"They do so now, but they were not much unlike yourself. Village folk, simple farmers, or maybe even merchants in places between here and there. They would not choose to live like this, in tents or under the stars, behind a wall that is clearly not enough to stop what haunts them." Ulric pointed so that Basimick could see the injured inside the makeshift hospital tents where flies swarmed in clouds and blood soaked rags dried in the sun. "They flee from their own war. Refugees that were lucky enough to survive where they were from, but unlucky enough to end up here."

"Are the elves so merciless that they would attack everyone?"

"Elves? No, these are not the victims of the elves. The Empire is at war with the orc. Everyone everywhere is at war with the orc. There is no elven war that anyone in Nhearn yet knows of. No one except you."

Basimick leaned back into his seat with thought. "I don't know much about the world," he admitted honestly.

"You have not seen much, but you are wise to acknowledge that truth. You have a passion to help others, this is also true, Basimick. Do not lose your desire to help, just like your kind father did before you, but do not be blind to the truths of Nhearn." Ulric looked at Felceon and frowned with Basimick, "The elves will not come here. I would boldly argue that there is no use in it for them. Felceon is exactly what you see now, important once in its prime, but no longer.

It is just a glorified horn bearer to the city if ever there were an alarm to be raised. The elves will pass here and move on to deal with whom they have grievance."

"Would the Empire help the dwarves, Ulric? I was sent to get help, you know."

Ulric was silent a moment as the carriages passed under the gatehouse on the western side of Felceon. "The Empire is preoccupied. I do not think they will help their allies when they consider what threats they already contend with."

"But would the elves attack the city in Presons?"

"If what you know of the elven army is true, and they are amassing in those woodlands, then there is a chance that the Imperial colony out there will be a target that the elves would seek to destroy. Perhaps it would be to remove anyone residing there from warning the dwarves, or maybe they would do nothing and move on without any interest of that place at all." Ulric leaned away from the window and looked at Basimick. "If you are going to help anyone, you must try to see the true purpose in things. I think that you could help a great many people someday."

CHAPTER XV
ARRIVING TO IMITHEON

The caravan had traveled a while further from Felceon, at last rounding the mountain ridge that protected passage westward. The tall gray stone stretching southward into the Great Plains from the Cragged Mountains no longer blocked the coming view of the valley ahead. Ulric shook Basimick from a slumber and waited for the young hunter to wake fully before pointing his attention out the window of the carriage. "If there is anything for you to see for the first time it should be the Snake Road. It is the only way to get to the high city of Imitheon, at least any path that we know of."

He rubbed his eyes and leaned into the window to see ahead of the caravan. On the north side of the great valley was a great wall that was sheer for a whole distance into the sky. The incredible cliff rested between the two ridges of the Cragged Mountains, the one to the east that had been pushing against their road, and another that mirrored the Felceon barrier as it reached toward the lands far into the west. Basimick adjusted his eyes and he could see other carts and gatherings of people scaling the stone rise with ease. Across the massive cliff wall was a carving of a road that switch backed at a leisurely grade all the way to the lip of the plateau above. To either side of the winding path of the Snake Road were towers that guarded it. They were both made of large white bricks and cut so that there were harsh angles to gaze at all directions of the valley. The two towers were built to the height of the plateau and they appeared to lean against the cliff face as though the whole mountain were crafted in the likeness of an Imperial planned defensive wall.

The carriages turned off from the Trade Road which continued toward the western arm of the mountains and the caravan began to climb the side of the cliff up the Snake Road. As they began the incline Basimick leaned forward so that he could see more of the road. He was surprised that the solid rock had been carved so that at least two carriages at a time could pass each other with enough space for comfort to mind the unprotected cliff edge. The horse and oxen pulling on the carts did not have to struggle to make the journey toward the summit, and the carriages traveled smoothly across the stone which seemed to be kept comfortable and clean, unlike some of the distances across the rutted Trade Road dirt.

It took most of the day to climb the Snake Road to the summit of the Imitheon Plateau and when they arrived Basimick was reinvigorated with a curiosity for the holds of the Empire. Around the plateau was a crown of sharp gray rises to match the granite faces of the entire range of the Cragged Mountains. The carriages pulled away from the cliff edge and followed the road toward a narrowing valley as the mountains continued to rise even further into the sky. Ahead of them was a canyon several distances deep that curved out of view. The mountain ridges to either side of the road held onto heavy mists and further hid the flat lands of the valley.

The carriages did not stop, though the road had once again become dirt as crop fields sprouted from cliff to cliff with only the road denying any land for their use. As they continued further into the deepening valley, the windows of the carriage at last could witness the city.

Basimick smiled with awe as the whole city unveiled itself from behind the curve of the valley. Imitheon was a wondrous place. The outer wall was built of white stones that had been stacked between the gray cliffs of the narrowing valley and the silhouette of the buildings were made impressively tall as their construction crawled up against the side of the sharp gray slope. As the clouds parted, the many turrets along the terraced streets revealed their true heights. The towers of Imitheon could oversee the way through the valley, their gaze perhaps could see beyond the mountains, beyond the cliffs, perhaps even beyond the horizon of the southern grasslands. Where the head of the caravan arrived was the main gate of the city and Basimick could see that the wide threshold could fit three carts abreast through the wall that could have been ten heights to the guards manning the parapets above.

Along the wall were banners, huge flags that were hung over the ramparts so that their tassels ended near the mid height of the wall. "Those are the houses of nobility," Ulric said as he discovered Basimick's curiosity towards the many symbols. He began to name them, but Basimick could not keep up to recall the lengthy list of people with two names. To either side of the main gate were banners of the city, a circle split by a wide line that was filled on its bottom. "The setting sun," Ulric continued to offer Basimick some information. "Imitheon is the western city of Midland and watches the setting of the day, where Armontrosia, which is the eastern city, hoists the same flag in reverse, as they watch the rising sun."

As the main entry opened to allow the Red Circus passage, the first cart was halted by a number of city authorities who were armed like Legion soldiers. A ranking member among them, whose left pauldron was marked in a copper hue, stepped up to the driver and asked, "For what purpose does this caravan enter this place, the Sister City of Imitheon?"

A murmur began outside of the carriage and Ulric smiled at Basimick as though he knew what the commotion was already about. Ulric's carriage driver knocked upon the roof as the head carriage driver loudly begged for pardon from the guard so that the master of the troupe could speak for them. "This is merely the common formality when entering the cities," Ulric said as he stood up and readied his attire before opening the door. "I am sure there is much more history to discuss, but if you would pardon me for business reasons." They both stepped out from the carriage, marched along the train of the Red Circus, and as they neared the head of the caravan he held a hand out for Basimick to wait nearby.

Lin appeared beside Ulric from between the carriages and he began to whisper something as they walked out of Basimick's earshot. He gently pointed back toward the rear of the caravan, but was quickly silenced. Master Reddon stopped only for a moment and glared at Lin before they both began again toward the guards of the city.

Ulric arrived at the gate confidently, a wide smile upon his face, his voice invitingly friendly, and he bowed properly to the authority so that the captain could repeat the inquiry of entry. "We are but traveling entertainers who had success in the Brother City of Armontrosia. We are the Red Circus and we hope to entertain the denizens during these trying times."

The guard captain scanned across the gathering membership within the gateway, "Any warrants or vagabonds? We wouldn't risk any compromises here in the city."

"Understandable, and we have none. You are welcome to check on each, though some of our members have come from afar and others may have been beyond the borders of the Empire from where they hail."

The captain watched as Ulric whistled and from the carts came a horde of youth to join the already large group at the gate. "Check," the captain ordered to his team of guards and they scattered among the throng to begin proper Imperial documentations.

As the captain prepared for his own duties Ulric paused him, "There is one guest I should mention before we begin all the official checks however."

"We appreciate the honesty," he was sure to reply in a rehearsed fashion. "Who is it?"

"Basimick," Ulric called and he stepped out through the members of the Red Circus.

The captain began to stutter, "A dragon hunter? What are you doing here?" Worry captured the attention from most of the guards as the captain begged Basimick for answers.

"I am not here for dragons," though Basimick knew that Olag was near to this city, his thoughts suddenly swaying just across the Imitheon Valley into Montontra, but Ulric hid a wink at him to avoid that detail. "I was rescued by these folk. If they can be treated well, please do so."

"By your word, master hunter, of course," the lead authority agreed.

"And if I may go to council for my own purpose," Basimick added.

"Immediately, sir."

Ulric grabbed Basimick by the shoulder, "This is where we must part for the moment. Nhearn is a small place. I am sure that in a way or in another we shall reunite, master hunter. Go with what luck I can give you, but heed my warning that any help you are seeking for others will need to come from you alone. Hope for much, but expect little, Basimick, son of Bassar."

"Thank you," Basimick hugged the tall man. "I would have been killed if lesser men had found me, or at least lost if they hadn't."

"You have repaid me well with pleasant company, and by rescuing an Emperor's hunter I will still be rewarded kindly to be sure."

"Good luck, Ulric Reddon."

"Good luck, Basimick."

Before the guard captain was able to get the attention of the dragon hunter, Basimick stopped by Lin and the guard responsible for checking his identity stepped aside. "Thank you for waking me and for all the conversation over the long distances. If ever there was someone I have met that I would like to meet twice," Basimick held out his hand as the words of their parting failed to come out.

Lin went for a hug and Basimick was happy to answer it. "We will meet again, friend. Just be careful around dragons, stay out of the grass, and you shouldn't have much of a hassle."

The two separated and Basimick waved for a moment to say farewell to the other members of the Red Circus. The captain of the guard then took Basimick across the busy gate plaza into the city proper, offering to guide him to the royal courts where he might accomplish his goals.

Another of the many guards came to Ulric and assumed command as the captain's leadership was removed from the gate. "Are there plazas where we may set up," Ulric was quick to seize the advantage of the shift in power. "Good spots for the crowds, somewhere spacious perhaps. Anything will do, but we can avoid all the extra formality of the city's responsibility. We are all rather weary of the road and I might not pry much for the reward of rescue that the city owes us if we could be allowed in more swiftly." Ulric winked at the guard who became flustered with the new position, "After all, a dragon hunter is worth quite a lot to the Emperor."

CHAPTER XVI
MEETING WITH THE KING

Basimick went into the city, climbing higher as it rose against the mountain slope, and he looked to either side of the street as he wandered. The houses were built of solid stone bricks and held together with mortar. There were many sets of stairs that led up to dwellings which were stacked upon each other over five heights directly upward, and some of the dwelling towers had rooftop parapets with bridges to terraces even higher in the city. It seemed that each of the labyrinth ramparts were watched by city guards, each of them armed in iron raiment with swords and halberds to match with one another in appearance. The alleyways, tower stairs, and switch back streets made passage confusing for Basimick, especially as columns of soldiers moved about while crowds of city folk meandered in and out from the shared trails and passages.

Crowded was all he could think. It was far more crowded than Ovelclutch had been, but still none of the citizens dared bother the dragon hunter, just as the dwarves had kept their distance back in the market ring. He could at times hear whispers of their concern, many wondering if there might be dragons near the city.

He looked over his shoulder and found that even the quick walk away from the city gate had gotten him well over the obstruction of the city wall in elevation.

From the middle of the street he could see through the farmland valley, over the ridge as it curved with the road, all the way to the crest of the plateau whose edge was like a horizon that fell onto the Snake Road, and beyond were the Great Plains, where at a great distance away was the true horizon of the land which disappeared into clouds that had gathered in the far south.

He returned his attention to the street and followed it to a corner where the way twisted back up against the slope and rose toward the opposite side of the city. He paused for a moment and his eyes stared toward the west, captured by the sudden sight that seemed to be missed by everyone around him. Where he stood upon the mountain, from the city plaza at the western point, the obstacle of the Cragged Mountain cliffs had ended, revealing the incredible view from the height of the mountaintop, and the city peered down into the hills of a vast farmland where he could gaze all the way out to the West-Gate Sea.

Basimick was so distracted by the vistas that he did not notice when a man had traded places with the dragon hunter's chaperone. The stranger began to walk beside Basimick as he continued along the street and the man kept pace beside the hunter for a while before speaking, "Well met, hunter." Basimick flinched with surprise and the stranger laughed a moment. "I would have thought you'd noticed me, but I was mistaken. I am sorry that I sent your guard away, but I would hope to meet with you for a moment without the common authority."

With some worry Basimick eyed the man carefully. The man's hair was only beginning to gray, he wore a fine chain shirt beneath a well-made black tunic that had been sown with a white embellishment of the Imperial crest that was presented proudly over the man's chest. He was well armed also with a quality sword at his waist and a shield which he bore upon his back. Metal guards were over his shins and forearms, but he only wore leather gloves and tall boots, unlike the guards of the city who wore metal gauntlets and iron plated shoes. "Who are you, sir?"

"Show me your mark and then I will answer thee."

"My mark?" Basimick reached into his pocket and took out the hunter's token in hopes that he was making the right gesture.

"A genuine dragon hunter. One of the Emperor's chosen."

"And you?"

"I am an Imperial Knight," he bowed at the waist and presented a heavy coin much in the likeness of the dragon hunter's token. Upon it was a sword defending a shield, and the other side had the inscription of the Emperor's commandments for this man's authority. "I am a chosen warrior, selected by the Emperor himself. I act on his behalf, but I am responsible to uphold his honor also, just as you are chosen to hunt the great beasts in his stead. Please, master hunter, if I may ask, is your business regarding dragons this hour?"

"I have knowledge of such things," Basimick said hesitantly. "But I am here to help bring news to the Empire and avoid any more loss of life."

The knight was worried about the dreadful news that the hunter carried. He quietly questioned, "Dragon?"

"Elves, sir. They destroyed the city of Ovelclutch and I have heard that they now move toward Presons."

"Ovelclutch? If that place fell I would wonder what consequence could befall us. It is one of the few places of respite along the Marching Road for the Legion, and also a place of defense against the hordes of orc in the Badlands, should it come to that. This news may mean that I need to take my attention away from the south."

"What is your business," Basimick asked kindly.

"Orc, for the moment. The war bands have become more frequent of late across Midland. The endless war takes a lot of our time and focus."

The pair of them had spoken for very little time, but Basimick found that the knight had led him all the way to the topmost terrace of the city. Before both of them was a courtyard of white stone and into the side of the gray mountain was a grand doorway carved like a palace building. It was an elaborate and welcoming facade, an impressive use of the towering cliff face.

"Politics are not my expertise," the knight chuckled to ward off what dread they both carried. "I assume it is not your realm of preference either, master hunter. Be courteous and firm, but expect little. Those that dwell in these halls are practiced naysayers. I wish you luck and offer you the first jab at whatever council awaits us inside." The knight waved Basimick to the doorway into the palace courts. "If we go at once, or if you go second, you may find them to be less agreeable."

"Thank you," and Basimick went across the royal yard to the large door.

"For Emperor and Empire, master hunter."

Basimick walked slowly through a wide corridor that was filled with decorum beyond the craft of mere masters and he entered through a grand threshold into the great hall of the palace. The massive chamber was well lit by many ornate chandeliers that dangled from the high ceiling above, as well as by numerous flaming sconces along the walls. There were also several large crackling hearths that filled the room with a welcoming glow and a comfortable warmth. Basimick thought of how much time he would need to take at the chopping stump to make enough kindling for such use, but he remembered that whoever was waiting for him within was wasting this fuel for the sake of appearance and this was the kind of person that he must confront.

At the opposite side of the regal room, across the glossed marble floor tiles, and up a single step, was the steward's chair. It was positioned to the left of the royal stage, and two steps above that was the king's grand throne in the center of the rise. Basimick's footsteps echoed in the cathedral-like chamber as he traveled toward the thrones. He gazed up and the ceiling was some ten heights above him, carved with such skill as to make the sound of breathing tenfold.

"Glorious, is it not?" A man uttered from the highest step before resting into his regal throne after quietly arriving from an unknown portal. He gently placed his hands over the arms of the king's throne so that the rings of his fingers were on display and the gems glimmered in the light of the many dancing fires.

"I have not seen much, it would seem," Basimick said slowly and deliberately. He had been bold in thinking the deed of speaking with nobility so easy, and he was nervous now before the king of Imitheon.

"Welcome to my city and within my borders, master hunter," the king waved his hand and bowed in his seat just enough that the gesture might be noticed. "I am the king of Imitheon, Lord Alistaire Bonnet, head of nobility within the House Bonnet. I am acting power and advisor to all of the dealings and concerns within the city and county of Imitheon." Alistaire leaned into his glorious throne with an air of smugness. "At times I may even speak with the weight of the Emperor's authority."

Basimick stood at the base of the kingly stair, standing center before the throne, and he faced the king directly. "Sir, I have news of great urgency."

"A dragon hunter comes to Imitheon with news of great urgency. I would believe it to be news regarding dragons."

"Yes," Basimick agreed with the king and he hesitated before continuing his thought. "Though dragon whereabouts is not the news that I have come to share, that I need to share. Elves have attacked Ovelclutch. They destroyed it. The armies of the elves are moving north and will be here soon. They intend to gather in Presons before they war with the dwarves."

"This is devastating news," the king brought the tips of his fingers together. After a long moment he continued, "It requires a great deal of thought and council."

"The dwarves need help. Presons may need help."

Alistaire nodded and looked at the empty seat two steps beneath his platform. "Dwarves?" He continued to nod as his gaze slowly fell upon Basimick once again. "The Empire of course enjoys our peace with the tradesmen of dwarven countries." King Alistaire held for another moment with deliberate thought, "And we also have treaties with the elves, elves of all sorts in fact. Woodland and grassland alike. A new enemy would be," he paused to think of the proper word, "taxing."

Basimick stared at the king of this Imperial city and was unsure why the choice to help wasn't an immediate *yes*.

"The Empire, the dwarven kingdoms, and the dominion of elves are spent on the ceaseless war with the orcs. They come from all places and attack with vigor against all things. Armed soldiers, unarmed peasants, women, children, beast, and babe. All the cities of the Empire, from Tronia to here in Imitheon which sits at the very Mouth of Montontra, the refugees of the Midlands come, and they are only the lucky few who have survived what horror chased them from their places.

"The garrisons of the Sister City are stretched, the armies of Armontrosia are dealing with the same conflict in the east, and Tronia, wherever they may be, claims to watch the pass to Southrunn. If we took another adversary, especially one who is one of the few friends we have in this great conflict, we risk the safety of the entirety of Midland, nay, the entire Empire itself." Alistaire appeared saddened, but Basimick could see that the king's demeanor wasn't genuine. "The township of Presons is an Imperial hold; perhaps the elves will remain our ally and continue north toward dwarf country should their business not be satisfied with that trade city. We cannot, however, send a garrison to defend a handful of distant citizens and risk this city to the monsters that already pilfer this county."

"What should be done," Basimick wanted an answer. "Who could help them? I must find help. The dwarves-"

King Alistaire leaned forward to appear sympathetic, but his eyes gave away his intentions. He was tired of dealing with this *petty* situation. "If you were to tell me that a dragon was heading to Presons I would encourage an Imperial dragon hunter to direct their attention to that woodland. It would only be proper that as an Emperor's chosen hunter you would lend yourself to that type of business instead of forcing an audience from leaders who are charged with so much more than you realize. If you were to slay that beast and then find yourself some time to shy away from your designation then perhaps you could waste your usefulness defending that place from a whole army of elves by your lonesome." The king's face twisted with irritation as he rested back into his throne. "Please, I am very busy with much," and with a wave of his hand a palace guard appeared beside Basimick. With the utmost insincerity, Alistaire called out to the Basimick as he left the kingly hall, "Best of luck in your travels, Emperor's dragon hunter."

Basimick left the royal hole in the side of the mountain. Guards that he had not seen upon entering were opening each door for him as he passed. The afternoon mists of the Cragged Mountains were crawling up the slopes so that the view below the courtyard into the terraces of the city became blocked and only the tower spires that were tall enough to match the highest tier of the city appeared aloft in the clouds. He stared at the sweeping current, the mountain fog swirling with the cold breeze as it flowed to follow along the city path in the direction of streets and avenues. He was very distracted, deep in thought, and he jumped when a heavy leather hand patted him on the shoulder.

"Sorry, master hunter."

Basimick turned and bowed when he discovered the knight beside him. "You just caught me off guard," he tried to make light of the shock.

"How was your talk? I know I told you to have no hope, but I still carried some for you."

"Not well, sir. There is no help coming."

"My talk went very similar to your own. The southern city will not receive aid. The Empire of Midland must be strong, each city and state able to stand on its own." He smiled briefly and let his true feelings of dismay show on his face. "I fear what will come next."

"What is next," Basimick asked as they both stood at the edge of the grand terrace and got lost in the motion of clouds together.

"I foresee a war without end. My heart tells me that much more evil will come, but the orc may only be the first of many such challenges." The knight shook his head, "Perhaps I am wrong. So long as the Empire has people like us, master hunter, there is a bit of hope left at least, even if only among us."

"Where are you going?"

"South, back to Tronia, may she still stand. I will go alone and with disappointment. Where will you go, master hunter? Home? Nay. Are there still dragons about?"

Basimick could still see the distant silhouettes of the dark volcanic mountains across the Imitheon Valley south where the dragon Olag of Fire might be recovering from his wounds. "I do not have a home to return to," he said after a while. "There is still a dragon to hunt," he gripped his sword and found that he was angry. "I suppose that is what the Empire wants of me." He had no home, his only companions were gone, his quest for help had ended with failure, and he had nowhere to go except where the duty of the Emperor commanded. *My father would hunt the dragon. Honor would have demanded that Bassar do so, no matter how hopeless his task was.* Basimick was obligated to go into Montontra on his own honor, to try his appointed task against all odds, for he was a dragon hunter of the Empire.

"I wish you luck in your travels and I wish us plenty more chances to meet. At least we were able to do so here, master hunter." The knight crossed an arm over his chest and bowed deeply with utmost respect.

Basimick returned the bow, practicing the crossed arm to return the courtesy, and they both smiled as best they could manage. The knight put the toe of his boot to the street behind him, turned ceremoniously in place, and left the plateau of the palace. Not once did he turn back to see Basimick again, and he faded away into the mountain mists of Imitheon. When he was ready, Basimick looked once again at the great palace doorway, frowned at the facade with disappointment, and left the plateau into the swirling clouds of the city streets.

CHAPTER XVII
AN ASSAULT AGAINST EVIL

Ulric had the Red Circus drive the carriages into the higher terraces of Imitheon and the city guards showed them the way to an old forum that sat vacant in the deep east districts. It was a wide arena nestled into a mountain narrow within the eastern cliff face. There was enough room to raise the pavilion there and most of the city would be able to see the red canvas of the tent's highest point.

The Red circus did not take long to fully occupy the arena and, as Ulric often allowed when they had entered a larger city, the waning hours of the day were given to the youth. Ulric appeared ragged and spent by travel, but he took a moment to personally meet with each member of his circus. To most he gave a handful of sovereigns, but as he came to the gifted, those of his inner membership, he offered a handful and a handshake with a little extra coin hidden from the newcomers. "First Night," he said to each youth as though it were a common term. "Enjoy the city, spend your coin, spread the word of the shows to come with tomorrow's daylight, and stretch your legs." Once the red banners were hung at the forum entrance the Red Circus disbanded for the evening to celebrate First Night.

Mebruk lifted an old pillar slab and moved the heavy brick to the gate of the arena. He set it down gently, but it still shook the ground as it fell from his grasp to rest. "For you, juggler. A stage. Is not so big, but up in the front like you like, aye."

"Maybe soon you can come into the big tent and dance around under my rope," Kalara laughed as the majority of the group released from the pavilion and rushed away toward the city.

Hilde smirked as she took a jab at the ropewalker to defend her juggler, "He tosses knives and you want him beneath your act?"

Hilde prepared to continue, but Haurus pulled her in under his arm. A jester at heart, he ignored Kalara's attempts to get a rise from him, and he spoke with the large man instead, "Give me a simple stump, Mebruk, smaller and off to the side. The main acts would be ashamed if the people thought the main show was just outside of the tent."

"Ulric wouldn't like you giving away a free show. No coin in it, right Haurus?" Lin appeared from the passing crowd of newer stock and nudged his friend under the ribs.

Kalara took a bow, "Tomorrow I shall be in the tent, as for tonight I will find the closest tavern."

"Stay safe," Hilde reminded her from Haurus' embrace, and she said it loud enough that it was meant as a warning to everyone else too.

"Of course, I couldn't be safer," and Kalara looked up at the giant Mebruk.

"She offer to pay from First Night coins," he smiled wide. "I am hired bodyguard now. I can tell this to Ulric, he hire me next when he go out."

Both of them laughed as they wandered into the foggy city night. Lin attempted to pass into the city also, but Hilde reached out and caught his sleeve. "I'd hate to take your attention for First Night, Lin, but we need to speak with you."

"I was hoping to find Basimick before he left or I was too busy with the circus. I don't know if anyone actually invited him to one of the shows before he went off."

"Told you not to talk too much with that hunter," Haurus smiled, though a great weight rested on him beneath the charade. "You'd get attached."

"What can I do for you both?"

Haurus and Hilde looked at each other before she spoke, "You weren't at the rest of the ritual on Last Night."

"Well, I-"

"You were there just when the box came in," Haurus said. "And then you reappeared when the box went out."

Lin nodded, unsure what was coming next.

Hilde then asked, "Do you know what is in that box?"

"Mirrors, I think, but I haven't seen anything else."

"Did you ever make a wish, Lin?"

"No. A wish? Ulric has taught me how to care and such for his mirrors. What soaps to use, how to keep the wood cured on the box, stuff like that. He did say that he will show me how to perform small rituals soon, but nothing about wishes or things of that nature."

Haurus reached out and held Lin's shoulder. "Do you know what it is?"

"No," Lin nervously laughed. "A priest's tool. It's just an altar or something like that."

"Evil," Hilde let him know. "Evil lives in the black mirror. Ulric said it was a god, a power that could change how the world worked."

"I've handled that crate and I have never felt any power in it."

Hilde began to tear and Haurus held her closer. "I was able to give my soul to Hilde, but she gave hers to the mirror."

"I wouldn't have if I had known."

Lin could not stand seeing anyone upset, but especially he could not bear Haurus and Hilde in any amount of sadness. He looked at the city, torch lights glaring through the mists. "I think I will see Basimick again someday. I'm pretty sure he would be disappointed to see me if I chose him over helping you two."

"Traveling with him made you better, Lin." Haurus hugged Hilde tighter. "Honor, duty, and goodness. I think he will make a good dragon hunter."

"Probably why Ulric never bothered to invite Basimick himself," Lin thought aloud. "If I help you-"

"Kalara can have my stump at the front door," Haurus tried to joke through the seriousness.

Lin nodded, knowing that he meant to leave the circus once it was done. "Do you think I could be a hunter?"

"We were going to travel."

"Already planned it out?"

Haurus nodded and Hilde offered, "You can come with us, Lin. We wouldn't want to leave you here."

"Where would we go?"

"Anywhere from here."

Lin looked at the red pavilion. "How many others know?"

"No one." Haurus frowned at last. "You were the only one that we could think to trust."

"And it has to be tonight," Lin kept his eyes on the crimson tent.

"I wouldn't ask it of you twice."

"You don't have to," Lin grabbed Haurus' hand. "Honor, duty, and goodness."

Haurus shook Lin's hand, "Honor, duty, and goodness."

Hilde wrapped herself around both of them, "Honor, duty, and goodness."

They waited for everyone to leave for the celebratory First Night before they quietly reentered the east forum. All three approached the edge of the grand pavilion before Lin separated from them to go about his task. He crept through the immense red tent, across the mysterious pit of sand that was not there before the tent had been raised, and he paused for a moment to look around. There weren't any props that had been set out for the shows in the morning. He had never thought of the tent supplies before, for it had not been something he had ever needed to think of. The openness of the Red Circus pavilion became terrible, but Lin went across the vast space without issue.

From the opening on the far side he found all the caravan carriages nestled against the mountain wall. The tent was filling the arena and it separated a private space from the city for their caravan that now felt like a very deep pit, the tent rising up as tall as the cliff side to block all view except into the fog above. He crept silently and saw there were still many members in the camp who had chosen to avoid the night of revelry, perhaps keeping their earnings for another time to get rest from traveling instead. Lin continued, none taking notice of him, and he reached the personal carriage of Ulric Reddon at the farthest distance within the narrow crevice of the arena pit.

He reached up and pulled the carriage door open quietly with a well versed hand, pulling at just the right speed to avoid the slow grinding of the hinges or the squeaking stress of the mechanisms if he had yanked with a quicker pace. Inside was Ulric, asleep. Days of travel and nights of entertaining the dragon hunter had consumed him to exhaustion. Lin reached into the traveling bed chamber and tugged upon Ulric's cape. Gently, to avoid pulling on Ulric himself, Lin lifted the folds and made a deliberate grab into one of the many pockets lining the inside of the fine cloth.

He pulled out a ring of keys, nearly one hundred metal tongs held upon it, and he lifted it away from Ulric without a hint of noise. He lowered the cape over his master like a blanket, closed the carriage door with the same practiced speed, and backed away from the narrow crevice of the arena. As the pavilion's rear entry came into view, Lin could see Haurus and Hilde waiting at the threshold. He turned away from them and went to the stacks of crates that the circus had unpacked throughout the afternoon. Among the many that were there he collected *the one*. It did not stand out from any other crate, many of the wooden boxes happened to be locked by many irons as well, but it did not for a moment stall Lin from selecting the right one. He pulled it away from the stack and placed it onto a small cart to avoid the sound of dragging it through the camp.

Lin returned to them and Haurus came to assist with the box, but Lin waved his hand to stop him. "I wasn't sure why before, but Ulric and I are the only ones to carry it. Wouldn't want it to start doing something now." As he entered the empty red tent, Haurus and Hilde followed behind him. The three gathered together in the mysterious sand at the middle of the pavilion and stood around the crate in which the black mirror resided. Lin looked at Haurus, "Are you sure that is what he said?"

"Absolutely," Haurus nodded with an uncharacteristically somber voice.

"If you know how to open it," Hilde tugged on Lin's tunic.

"He never told me what it was, just how to care for it. He wanted me to take his place someday I think." Lin looked up from his knees at Hilde, "I thought of him as a father."

"We all did," she nodded.

"Do you have the keys? Do you know the combinations?" Haurus begged Lin.

"What do you think everyone else will do when they know what we did," Lin was hesitant.

Hilde shook her head knowing that the others might not understand. As she remembered what had happened in Armontrosia, she thought perhaps that they didn't care now that they were granted their wishes. She looked Lin in the eyes and repeated, "Honor, duty, and goodness."

Haurus reached out and touched Lin's shoulder, "We would not serve such evil willingly. Ulric is a trickster. We sold our souls for gifts, the price of which we knew nothing about."

"Do it, Lin," Hilde begged.

He began to open the crate. He pulled out the collection of keys held upon a metal ring and picked out a specific key from the hundred or so. He faced the crate so that the two locks were toward him and then he stepped aside to unlock one of the other side irons. Lin then moved in such a way that he appeared to be afraid of the crate. He unlocked the first iron before going to the opposite side where he pulled a different key from the ring and then removed the next lock. He kneeled at the front of the crate and took two other keys for the final front irons. He separated the two halves of the crate and his gaze met his reflection in the black mirror as it rested into the sand. Lin's eyes moved to the silver mirror as he set it down gently and with worry his gaze went back to the abyss where his face was no longer like his own.

"Servant boy?"

The voice that arrived from nowhere was unexpected and he fell backwards into the sand with fright. He had never before seen anything out of the ordinary within the box, but it had revealed itself to him now and whatever it was spoke as though it knew him, as though it had been watching him each time he had handled the crate. Shocked, he looked at the other two, but their gaze was fixated on the rear entry of the pavilion.

From the rear threshold, toward the encampment of the Red Circus, he came. Ulric Reddon shouted as Lin rose up his arm and slammed his closed fist into his own twisted reflection that stared back towards him from the black mirror. With blood dripping from his fingers Lin began frantically reaching into the crate, "He cannot have it! Grab it all! Go, go!" All three of them grabbed shards of the black mirror and blood dripped into the sand as they gripped the broken glass tightly. There were black shards left in slivers around the mirror's crate, but each had taken enough pieces that the vile portal could not be made whole again.

Ulric drew out a blade that none of them had seen before and he began to slash as he neared them. "Refuse children! Ungrateful beasts! Destroyers, all of you!"

"Lin! Lin, run!" Haurus revealed one of his many hidden blades and threw a dagger at Ulric who was stricken over the shoulder. Lin took hold of a final shard from within the crate and he escaped just in time to avoid Ulric's sword as it plunged into the ground. He tried to gain traction in the sand to flee further, but in a panic he stumbled and tripped several times, as though the pit were working against him.

"Duck, Lin!" The ball of fire swung over him and Ulric stepped back as Hilde spun the censer over them. She loosened her grip so the chain went further and further toward Ulric from her wounded hands. Lin stayed low beneath the swirling weapon, crawling as quickly as he could toward the pavilion's threshold into the city. He could feel the flames above him, the wild censer becoming an inferno as it raced around the room, but the shadow of the Red Circus pavilion seemed to overpower the light of Hilda's fire. The tent was closing in around him, but at last he escaped from the scarlet portal.

Haurus threw another blade and Ulric Reddon deflected it barely with a labored heave of his sword. The juggler ducked beneath the fine chain of the fireball and neared toward her. "Hilde!"

She caught the chain and pulled it close so that the metal ball spun quickly in tight circles overhead. The juggler and the dancer backed away from the broken crate while threatening to lash out at Ulric Reddon if he tried to stop them. They continued and were out of the doorway in moments, fleeing into the night. All three fled away from the arena circle, away from the immense tent that was looming over them, its shadow ominous and sinister in the haze of foggy city lights.

Lin ran as fast as he could from the arena pit ahead of the other two, afraid of retaliation from Ulric if he were to give chase, but he was fearful more so of whatever supernatural wrath that surely followed him. He could feel it gnawing, growing about him like a sinister vapor in the dark of the night. As he left the view of the encampment and arrived at the first city plaza, he was in such a panic that he crashed into a standing market stall where the sound of thousands of beads and buttons crashed across the street. Every single one of the pin drop noises was louder than a storm as Lin tried to regain himself. "On your feet," Haurus reached out his hand and pulled Lin upright as they continued to sprint downhill toward the city gate. Still incited by fear, they ran off into the lower streets of Imitheon and they made sure to disappear.

CHAPTER XVIII
THE PASSING OF EVIL

As morning came to the city of Imitheon, the Red Circus silently began to pack the pavilion and the members of the intriguing spectacle to the city had worked throughout the night to get the caravan of colorful carriages ready for departure. Within the city plaza where the street up toward the cliff side arena began, watching as the wondrous tent was being collapsed, was an elderly woman who was taking a break from bending over to gather her goods that had spilled all over the street. She was upset by the vandalism of her market stall, but she remained in good spirits as she leaned down once more to pluck the beads and buttons from the grooves of the tiled plaza, taking brief moments to stretch her tightening back and enjoy the sight of the circus that never got a chance to perform.

"Let me help you," a young woman said, already bent to pick up the furthest of the fallen beads.

"No need, dearie, no need," the elder attempted to politely wave the assistance away. "I would not burden a Temple mage with my effort."

"Tisn't a burden at all. It is the duty of the Mage's Temple to help others." She took hold of the red cloak uniform she wore with pride and bundled it in one arm so that it did not sweep across the ground to scatter the beads or block her view.

"At least let me know who is kind enough to help a lowly bead vendor," the elder put her hands on her hips and tried to relieve some of the ache from her back.

"I am Scholar Sarah, the apothecary," she lowered her head to offer respect.

They worked together silently for some time until Sarah had a handful of various jewelry and she poured it onto the countertop pan upon the market stall. The elderly woman moved to her proper side of the counter, sat on her crooked stool, and began to sort through her inventory. "You look like a familiar face."

"Have you seen me about the city? I wander through the markets on this terrace often."

The old woman dragged her arm across the stall to clear the counter of any debris to begin sorting and she winced as the pain in her back swelled up. "No, no. You mages come and go as you learn and move on from the city. They can all be seen by the color of their cloak when they wander, the gray and reds, all the same wandering the streets. I can see your face. I recognize it, I think."

"Oh I am sure that it must just be my duty with the apothecary, my Lady," Sarah began to sort the inventory into a wooden box that was partitioned in the fashion of a noble's jewelry drawer.

The elder leaned back and the stool creaked, the wood of the seat as aged as she was. "I see it now; you have a father in Dwarf Country, don't you?" She put a finger to her chin, "I have been alive too long perhaps, but if I knew it for sure I would say you are DiGardi."

Sarah laughed, "That is quite a trained eye. I do not suspect my father has come up the Snake Road for some time."

The elder clapped her hands together, "DiGardi."

"Sarah DiGardi," she bowed her head. "Though, that was before I took the Temple mantle."

"Ah, Sarah DiGardi. I do miss the good wheat your father brought. The miller does too, I am sure of that."

"Not too often I am called by my name."

"Oh," the woman nodded. "Sorry, child. I nearly forgot my manners. I am dealing with a Temple mage. Wouldn't want them to think you were breaking any of their rules now. What was your proper title now, dearie?"

"Scholar Sarah, but think nothing of it. I would still go by my name given the choice." The mage scholar was nearly finished organizing the pile when a shard of black glass came up and refused to be sorted in with the other beads or buttons. "What would you like to do with this one here?"

The elder carefully inspected the glass, thankful she had not grabbed it up with any bit of haste and accidently cut herself upon the edges. "I can make something very nice with this piece here," she made a smile so wide that it became infectious.

"I hope it helped-"

"Certainly did, Scholar Sarah," she was quick to reply

"I must be on my way now. My apologies, but an herb farmer is coming and the alchemists sent me to get a fresh supply."

"Well, be off then. Wouldn't want to hold the apothecary hostage. I get my poultice from the Temple after all," and she continued a lengthy anecdote regarding her tender back without inhale for some time.

Sarah smiled and bowed while backing away from the market stall.

"Said be off," the elder laughed.

The red cloak trailed behind her as she made her way to the lower city districts near the gates. The open mall between the wall and the first dwellings of the city was a flurry of activity as the plateau farmers brought the city the daily produce and vendors from beneath the cliff arrived to sell their wares from up the Snake Road. She weaved through the crowds, said hello to merchants she had become common with, and she arrived at the carriage of the herb farmer, the pouch of sovereigns already in her hand to trade with.

"You Temple folk make it easy," he laughed as he took the coins and passed the heavy bundle. "Meeting me at the gate too, I appreciate it."

"Easier to make the way down here from the Temple than to go all the way down to the valley."

"Snake Road ain't too bad this time of year. Temple buys enough to make the farm worthwhile. I do appreciate the connection, Miss DiGardi."

She frowned and heaved the heavy bundle up, "Of course. Anything to help out folk back home."

He put a hand over his chest, "I am so sorry, Scholar Sarah, I meant no offense if I called you out."

"Of course not. Just be more careful when we meet again. The Temple alchemists like having the supply and I wouldn't want to spoil that."

"Course not," the farmer bowed his apology. "Good day to you."

"Good day to you," she said before turning away to quickly leave the city front mall.

She spent more time among the markets, moving stall to stall, cart to cart, gathering specific items for the mages. She continued on well passed midday and her arms began to tire. At last she turned to climb back into the city, leaving the bustling plaza into the crowded streets. Sarah returned to the Mage's Temple that resided just below the top most terrace of the city, carrying the wrapped parcel of labeled herbs, bags of spices, and bouquets of specialty flowers that the other members of the apothecary were anticipating. She was prepared to open the Mage's Temple entry into the eastern cliff face, a golden doorway adorned with the watchful copper eye of the mage, when it suddenly opened on its own. "Scholar Sarah, very good." Another mage in a red cloak leaned into the Temple and shouted, "The delivery has come."

As she entered into the temple foyer a surge of red cloaked peers ravaged what they could of the herb supply, forcing it from her hands with wild excitement for what experiments could be done as she struggled to also close the door. They each thanked her repeatedly as the parcels quickly dwindled away.

As she struggled with the door, another mage in a gray cloak came to assist her, and shut the Temple so that the sound of the city vanished. Her eyes seemed scolding as she looked at him, "Shouldn't you be getting these shipments, Reginald?"

He made an exaggerated shrug, "Gray cloaks have important tasks that go far beyond simply picking up and dropping off."

A smile crept over her as Reginald seemed prepared to joke with her, "Is that so, courier?"

"I am also allowed to listen here and to speak there when asked," he chuckled.

"That still sounds like couriering."

"Well if you feel that you would do better than I, red cloak, then I will not give you your delivery."

"What delivery?"

"A woman came by and dropped it off for you. She said you had helped her this morning and she insisted on thanking you. She even waited for a while, but the trip to the gate and back must have taken up some time."

"The delivery is at the gate at the bottom of the city. It would certainly be quicker if you used your mage skills to get it, gray cloak."

"She seemed overjoyed to have *just the thing* to thank you."

"I wouldn't accept a gift for helping clean up after a vandal knocked over a merchant's cart. I did it as an act of good will in good faith from the Temple."

"The Mage's Temple would normally agree with you and add it to our coffers, but the head mages met and have decided to allow you such a gift in this particular case."

"Well that is a strange exception."

"It was more that they did not want it to stay on Temple grounds." He pulled out a sizable wooden box hidden within the magical places of his courier's gray cloak and handed it over to Sarah. "Do as you wish with it, but keep it well away from everyone. It is such an odd thing. It hardly resembles a gift really."

It was a strangely made box. Very tall and thin, like a crate for a wine bottle, but the lid was hinged at the top so that the opening was wide enough that only fingers could reach in. Sarah attempted to pull something out and it felt like a burlap sack sewn tightly. "What is it?"

He shook his head, refusing to answer, waiting to unleash his laughter behind a tightly clenched lip.

Her fingers managed to grasp a corner of whatever it was and she began to pull it from the narrow opening of the box. As the head of it poked out she became haunted and the thing slipped away into the box again. She tilted the box so that light from the decorative glass in the Temple ceiling above could shine in. "It's just a bit surprising is all," she tried to hush Reginald's laughter.

Inside the box were two blunt hooks where the thing must have been caught under what appeared to be arms, but now it was slumped at the bottom of the box and seemed to be staring up at her. No longer willing to reach in and get it, she tilted the box and let the burlap thing slide out onto a table. It struck awkwardly on the rump and the weighted limbs of it moved about in a grotesque fashion. "It looks like a wicked little mandrake made from jute sack," Reginald chuckled again.

"Is it supposed to be a doll?" She picked up its lifeless body and the limbs were limply pulled downward with gravity. The gangly arms and lengthy legs were weighted at their ends so that they swung like pendulums toward the floor. Even its posterior was weighted so that the torso wagged about like a dead fish. For a mouth was just a simple row of stitches, each crisscross maneuvering over a straight line of thick dark twine. For the eyes were two buttons made from the strange black glass that had no matching pieces in the old woman's collection.

Sarah found a brief letter scratched onto a bit of parchment that must have fallen out onto the table with the doll. It read:

Mr. Buttoneyes very much enjoys nice deeds and will help you by eating any of your bad thoughts. For you to keep for your kindness, Scholar Sarah.

She was relieved that the letter wasn't made out to DiGardi and she stuffed the doll back into the box. "I must have made an impression on her."

"Certainly not as much as that doll has made an impression on us."

"She said she was a jeweler, or a bead maker."

"Those jet buttons seem well tooled."

"She must have made them today and sewn them onto this thing for me." Sarah sighed, "She could have just gotten rid of it."

"As far as any of us could tell it isn't magically cursed or anything, so whatever you wish to do with your doll," but the uncontrollable laughter returned before Reginald was able to continue his thought.

"I am going to be making a trip to the herb farmers in Dwarf Country passed Delceon. There are enough hills out there to bury it someplace."

"You wouldn't want a courier to venture in your stead?"

"I am an apothecary scholar," she pointed to the official pendant pinned to her red cloak. "Let me use some of my expertise. I need to see what other products we can get for the apothecary. I might even be able to see if the dwarves around there have anything for the alchemists."

"Well if you won't have a courier go with you, at least take my talisman for your journey. The Snake Road is long enough if you're going downhill." The gray cloak took out an iridescent stone that had a shimmering appearance of magic. "Moonstone, with just a bit of enchantment. Helps get you where you need to go in a hurry."

"Is that the gray cloak secret," Sarah laughed and took the stone from him.

"That? No, we have better secrets than that. When you know your heading just task the stone to go to the threshold. You should arrive at the gate of the city in a very timely manner, but then the enchantment should wear thin."

"Thank you."

"What are friends for? I have a bit of time here in the city before I would need it again anyway. Staying here for a bit will give me some time to meditate and enchant another."

"I will only be gone a few days I would guess. Probably a little less if I don't have to climb back up the plateau."

Reginald fought through a resurgence of laughter for a moment, "Just make sure to forget where you hid that thing so you aren't tempted to bring it back here."

CHAPTER XIX
ELMINIL AND LISSUANA

Elminil continued southward with his young ward beside him. They had some conversations about the landscape and as they came across sights worthy of mention the old elf would test her knowledge with a variety of questions which she answered excitedly. They walked quickly, their pace naturally faster than other travelers, and they wandered from the northern coasts into Imperial farmlands without noticing the many spans that had passed beneath their feet. Suddenly Elminil motioned for her to evade the sight of the road as something approached.

Even he ducked into the brush beside the road and together they hid as the travelers approaching rose over a hill into their view. Abigael stared at them quietly. They were loud, but they must not have needed to hide their presence as they marched northward. It was a large group of sylvari wood elves.

She studied them as they passed by their hiding place. The elves all wore armor and bore weapons, but she noticed that some of the equipment had been created by numerous craftsmen. The force marching along the road was sizable as well, though one of the elves had on a circlet crown that marked him as a noble of higher stratum, and the others that were about the noble elf must have understandably been a protective entourage.

Abigael was still, but she had been taught well, and her hiding spot allowed her to see most of the landscape unobscured. *Do not hide your sight while hiding yourself,* she remembered from one of her early lessons.

In the hands of the elven travelers were banners held high, something not typical of a random wandering band, but for royalty, this too wasn't extraordinary. They had long flags that whipped about on the breeze, ones that she recognized as the elves of the Northern Territories, and she spent a moment to recall the name of their dominion, but then figured that this detail would manifest itself eventually. Her interest shifted to the other banner, a large blank tapestry draped from a crossed metal bar. It was only white across its face and it was adorned with silver tassels. Her brow pinched as she recognized the origin and she risked moving to catch Elminil's reaction to the sight of it. He offered none.

As the elven battle host moved on, over the hills out of view from their own travel, they left their hiding place. "Mr. White-Waters?"

"Yes, Abigael?"

"Why would the wood elves carry a banner of the High Elves? Those flags don't exist any longer, right?"

"Not for almost three thousand years," Elminil glanced back up the road toward the north. "And they would have only been common three thousand years before that."

Abigael tried to think so that she could impress her teacher, and he remained quiet to allow her a chance to draw out a conclusion while he thought to himself. "Where do elves meet?"

"There are many places," Elminil returned as he always did when she asked a *bad question.*

"Where is the most important place for a royal elf to visit? Those wood elves are from across the Great Sea in the Northern Territories."

"From the dominion of Dol and Gor."

"Yes." Abigael frowned as the information to her forgotten trivia was freely given. "Where would they go?"

Elminil smiled as she asked a better question. "Krethnarok. Wood elves believe that forest to be the oldest on the face of Nhearn. They believe it may have been the forest where Walde resided."

"Walde," Abigael tried to think of the name. "Himmel's relative?"

"Of sorts."

Abigael thought to remind herself of those legends later and she kept her mind on the oddity at hand. "Who summoned who?"

Elminil was delighted. "Ah, that is a good question."

Abigael started beaming and she continued the investigation with excitement. "If Dol and Gor came to meet, then it must be a struggle in the Northern Territories. I believe that they would be concerned with the human colonies up there? But a war with the Empire, even colonials, would be bad."

"Why would this be bad?"

"Orc," Abigael answered. "The Imperial Legion keeps the orc controlled. Also they are allies, I think."

"Yes."

"So it is more likely that Krethnarok called for them to come."

"Yes," Elminil nodded with amusement as he too came to the same conclusion.

"Does Krethnarok use the High Elf flags?"

"No, they do not."

Abigael was surprised and her mind began to race. *There would be no reason for the sylvari to use the same colors and shape of the banners used by the Eternal Empire. The language is different. The religions are different. The histories are different.* "Are they imposters?"

"Perhaps. Emulating the old ways, perhaps."

"It is not a coincidence," Abigael said with surety.

"No." Elminil put a hand over his chin and thought.

It was clear to Abigael that even he was at a loss. They both continued on the road southward, wandering over stone bridges built by the dwarves and then maintained by humans. Abigael took all of this in and thought to test herself with Elminil's knowledge, but she continued to give him time to think to himself. After many more spans away from the elves, another traveler appeared.

"Mr. White-Waters," Abigael notified him, for she knew that when he became entrenched in thought he would also become unaware of his surroundings.

"You saw her," he asked.

"Yes," Abigael answered with hesitation.

"Impressive."

The approaching traveler dipped out of view as they entered into dales and then they would reappear on a closer hilltop than she should have. Abigael studied the stranger when she could. The traveler did not seem armed at all, a significant risk when wandering alone, the only exception being her thin and well-worn walking stick. The traveler had a heavy tome slung over her shoulder, the leather strap stitched to the spine of the book so that the cover opened as it hung and the pages fluttered with each step. Her shoes, as she got close enough to notice, were tattered from long distances of walking, which matched the appearance of the simple worn robe.

As the traveler neared she waved, doing so with such glee that it was unsettling for Abigael. Elminil patted his ward on the head, "She is a nice person. You may find her overbearing, but she is genuine."

Abigael nodded, but her guard was still high as the traveler rose up the road toward their own hilltop.

"Elminil of White-Waters," the traveler smiled so that her teeth were on display.

"Lissuana of the Watchers," he allowed the traveler a hug, which was a very rare gift to receive from Elminil.

"And who is this," Lissuana squatted while leaning on her walking stick so that she was at eye level to Elminil's young ward.

"I am Abigael," she said.

"A pleasure," the traveler put her hand out and Abigael shook it firmly in the Imperial fashion, which she assumed the stranger had done only because she was a human. "You can call me Lisa, if ever we meet again. I am sure that we will if you are truly Elminil's protégé."

"If that is so," Elminil put a hand on his ward's shoulder. "Then when you make note of her you may do so as Abigael White-Waters."

"My, what an honor," Lisa said, but Abigael thought the tone was patronizing.

"What are you doing, Lissuana?" Elminil stared at the traveling human. "Do you have something to do with the elves of Dol and Gor who passed us by?"

"No, but I may be concerned with them."

"If I recall, you were the one who meddled most often."

Lisa blushed, "No, it is not me this time. I could ask you the same though. It isn't very often that High Elven colors are flown these days."

Elminil surrendered a somber reaction and Lisa apologized quickly. He spoke with a grim raspy voice, "No, you were right to pry. It is quite the coincidence, them and I on the road together. It is true, after all, that those colors are not witnessed much now."

"Hey," Lisa smiled and tried to return to a jolly tone. "I think I am running a bit late for a meeting."

"Oh," Elminil tried to mimic the change in tone, but Abigael could tell that he was lingering on a dark thought.

"You wouldn't still happen to know the passage of the Stone Way, would you?"

"That was also many years ago now." Elminil took a heavy breath as he studied the mountains in the east. "Dwamaklad still looks the same, with all the same ravines that lead to empty passages." He pointed back toward the south where she had come from. "That cliff there, just north of the arm."

"Of course," she fixed the large book sling on her shoulder, gripped the walking stick with new vigor, and set forth toward the mountains. "Until next we meet, Elminil. Always a pleasure to encounter you along your way. And until we meet again, Abigael White-Waters."

As the strange wanderer departed into the untamed hills off the road, Abigael asked, "Who is she?" But

Elminil remained quiet. *That was a bad question,* she thought. "What is she?"

His smile returned, "Be wary of them, but they are never the same twice. There are others like her, though I find her to be the most pleasant company among their kind. You must be quick witted around them."

"Will they hurt me, if they could?"

"They are not supposed to."

That was not a comforting answer. She shifted the tone, "Why did you tell her to call me White-Waters?"

"Did you not want to be?" He smiled wide as she rebuked the notion. He laughed, "I am very proud of you. You will earn that name, Abigael. You have already," he put a hand on her shoulder as they continued southward. "And I know you will earn it for yourself too, in time."

CHAPTER XX
SARAH RETURNS HOME

Several days of travel away from the city and passed the western fortress of Delceon, Sarah made her way through the fertile fields of Dwarf Country back home. She marched into the hills and over the bridges where streams gently flowed toward the sea from the ravines of the dwarven cliff faces of Dwamaklad. At last she crossed over the final bridge where the stream marked the edge of the property and she entered into the expansive fields that had been recently plowed for the autumn wheat seeding. There was a spring in her step now that she was home and she crested the hill beside the banks of the stream. As the sight of the family manor revealed itself she was stricken by the sight and she stood frozen for a moment at the top of the hill.

She could see the smoke from a great distance and she used what energy she had left to quicken her pace across the property. There were no laborers across the land, no animals loose, and she couldn't see any other travelers on the road. As she neared the manor it became clear that the DiGardi home had been set ablaze. The stone wall that surrounded the manor's courtyard was containing the fire for the moment, but within was a cauldron fully engulfed by an angry flame. Sarah ran to one of her garden planters near the wall where she could step into the bed and peer over into the yard. As she stood on tip-toe her face was scorched by the heat and she recoiled. "Da," she cried out over and over, but there was no answer. Sarah went to the front gate and discovered that the metal handle had melted from within, the mechanisms seizing the door shut. "Da!"

She tried to kick the gate and she began frantically striking it until her knuckles were sore, yet it remained a barrier. What little hope that she had was waning quickly. She began shouting, crying for any passerby or god above to help her, but the home was entirely consumed. "Ma," she whimpered, but surely it was too late to rescue anyone left within.

Sarah fell to her knees and was shaking as the adrenaline was pulsing through her, exhausting her as thoughts of how to rescue anyone raced about her mind. She looked at the farmland around her in hope that her father might have been out trading across the streams when it had happened. She quickly realized that if he had noticed the smoke from any distance he would be there at the gate beside her and all hope was lost that her parents were still alive.

Sarah could not move her eyes to focus and had to move her whole body to gain a vantage of the family's plot of land. Away from the garden and across a field, atop a hill looking over the manor, was the barn, still untouched by the fire. The door into the barn was open, left ajar by usual suspects, and a surge of hope returned, her mind racing that perhaps her younger siblings might be alive.

She began to run, sprinting faster than she thought she was able, and to either side of the path she flung her belongings aside to hurry herself across the field to the open door of the large barn house. She crashed into the door and flung it open. Within smelled of smoke as the plume of the manor fire got trapped near the rafters, but she braved to go in. "Kate? William? Are you in here?" There was no answer. Her mind was quick to surrender and the dreadful realization of total loss washed over what hope she had remaining.

"Sarah?"

"William!" It was instant relief, as though nothing bad was happening or had ever happened before. Her brother was alive and she could see his eyes gazing down at her from up in the loft. "Come down, the smoke will catch you up there. Come on down. Don't be afraid, I am here now." She waved at him gently and went to the ladder to hold it steady. From the loft above, her brother stiffly came down, one step at a time, and she could feel him shivering with nerves as his hands gripped tight to the rungs. As he neared the bottom her sister Kate appeared and began down the ladder, though she was shaking worse than their brother. They both safely arrived on the ground and she gripped their hands to pull them outside into the fresh air. Sarah fell to her knees and her siblings were swiftly captured in a tight hug. "What happened? Be honest, please. Tell me, there is no trouble. I won't be mean. I promise." She rubbed William's head and drew Kate close so that they had to speak into each other. She locked eyes with William, "What happened?"

"We were in the house with Ma and she started to fade away-"

"Like she normally does," Kate added.

"But she made sort of a weird noise this time," William said.

"Like Da had told us about," Kate finished the thought.

"And I," but he became worried and tearful. His eyes became red and he buried his whole head into Sarah's cloak to hide.

"He blew up," Kate said solemnly.

Sarah shook her head and grabbed hold of him tighter. "What do you mean he blew up, Kate?"

"There was a fire."

"He started a fire," Sarah asked, but William was quick to shake his head and hide deeper.

"I don't know what it was," he sobbed and couldn't control the volume of his voice as panic and guilt overwhelmed him. "I didn't mean to do it! I don't know how I did it!"

"He blew up," Kate tried to reach out and hug her brother, but Sarah had her in too tight of an embrace for her to shelter William.

Sarah felt around her brother's neck, "Where is your necklace I gave you, the good luck one?"

He did not speak and Kate was quick to answer for him, "He tried to give it to Ma for good luck."

"And Da? Where was Da when this happened," Sarah softened her face as she realized she was being demanding, but Kate was silent, staring back at Sarah with a fearful look. Kate did not have to say what happened, it was plain to see in her eyes, and Sarah did not ask her again. "I need you to be brave right now, because I need to know this. It is very important. Do you understand?"

Kate nodded

"What did it look like, Kate? The fire."

"It came out from him. He blew up. The room just started burning. The floor, and then the chairs, and then the paintings, and the walls, and it, and all of the, uh,"

Kate seemed less able to speak as she tried to recall the horror of it. "William just blew up I think."

"I didn't mean it," he cried.

"No," Sarah wrapped her arms around their heads and cradled them both against her. "No, of course not. It isn't your fault, dear brother. It is nobody's fault." She rocked them both gently in an increasingly tighter embrace. "No one is to blame. It's just an accident, that's all."

They stayed just outside the barn for a while until Kate could no longer stand to be hugged and she pushed herself away. Sarah got up from her knees and stood tall over her younger siblings while she tried to think of what to do. "Stay here please." She moved William against the wall of the barn facing away from the manor to sit as his sobbing left him unable to remain up straight. "I will be back quickly and then we will leave. We don't need to stay here and there isn't anything that we need from the manor now," she reassured them.

Sarah left the barn and began collecting what she had discarded along the path. She crossed the field, her mind relieved that someone was alive, but as she neared the manor there came the truth that her parents were gone. She collected the things she had left beside the gate and stared at the handle that had melted even more since she had last seen it. She looked at the fire devouring the old courtyard oak and saw that it was made of a deeper hue than any natural blaze. It was most certainly magical.

She took a deep breath to settle her nerves. She placed a hand upon the warm gate and offered a gentle prayer for her mother to pass on into the Tower, congratulating her that her time of suffering had at last ended. For her father she kept her hand pressed to the gate and she stood up straight, staring at the metal doorway as though it were more significant than it had ever been before.

"We had talked about it, but I had hoped the day would come much later. I wished it wouldn't have come at all." She nodded as though she knew that her father was in agreement too. "I am sorry I wasn't here, Da. I will make sure that we don't get hurt anymore."

Her hand slid down the gate and fell to her side. She turned toward the barn and walked away from the manor, not bothering to check on the garden or look around for any keepsakes. The walk toward her siblings was fraught with planning. She moved automatically, but her mind was rapidly deciphering what to do next.

She returned to the barn and took William by the hand. "Come, we will leave now. We need to go before night starts coming on. We need to get a bit of distance while there is daylight and we can make camp to rest soon." Sarah motioned for Kate to follow as she took their brother toward the road. "No need to turn back and see it now. It isn't brave to look," but Kate was already looking at the fire and did not look away as they left toward the south.

Sarah could not control her sister and with William still in shock she had enough to struggle with. She would make deep sighs at times, but her breathing never recovered to an even pace. Her first thought was to go to the Mage's Temple in Imitheon, but she could not take them there. There was no room for them, no place to stay that she could trust in the city, and if the Temple mages discovered what it was that she knew about her brother the Auroran would inevitably come to take him away. The thought of losing him was too much to consider and she abandoned any plan to return to Imitheon. "There is a place in Bogramville that I have heard of," she said after hours of thinking. "It is a church that can take care of people like us. I will have to take us there until I can think of a more permanent solution, but it is a very long way from here."

"What about your city," Kate asked. "Da said it wasn't too far and that it was a nice city."

"I don't think Da has been to Imitheon for a long while, Kate."

"No," Kate sped up from behind to walk beside her siblings. "Do you need help, sis? I can hold something for you."

Sarah realized that she had been carrying a lot of packages in addition to holding onto her brother. She smiled as a distractingly happy thought crossed her mind. *Gray Cloak Reginald would be all over me with jokes and teasing about all these packages I've been trudging around with.* The thought was quick to pass, the smile arriving and fading in only a moment, but she knew such comforts would be needed to continue on in the dark times to come.

The three of them stopped for a moment so that Sarah could juggle with a package that looked like one of their father's special wine deliveries. "Here," she handed Kate the strange box and as she did a piece of shimmering stone fell to the dirt of the road. "Oh, thank you, Reginald."

While she picked up the moonstone trinket, Kate flipped the box around over and over to try and discover what was inside. With piqued interest she asked, "What is it?"

"It's a traveler's totem. A magic thing. It will help us get to Bogramville a bit faster." Sarah looked up after dusting the enchanted talisman on her cloak and saw that Kate was more curious about the box. "Oh, sorry. The box, it's a doll. I brought it here for you actually. You can open it if it would be easier for you to carry, Kate."

Her sister opened up the wooden box immediately and took the strange creature from the hanger hooks. It slumped into her arms and the gangly limbs were swinging loosely toward the ground. "It looks happy," she said with glee. She wrapped it into a tight hug and helped the doll get its long arms over her shoulders to get a hug in return.

"Happy," Sarah was unsettled by the flat line of the stitched mouth, but she did not want to dismantle any morale that her sister could take from the doll. "Very happy," she agreed at last. "His name is Mr. Buttoneyes, and you must take care of him with happy thoughts. That's what it likes to eat apparently."

Sarah took up her brother's hand again and rubbed the iridescent stone while muttering the destination she wanted to arrive at into the enchantment. Behind her, Kate continued to talk with Mr. Buttoneyes, but she needed to focus on putting her intention into the enchanted traveling totem. Kate looked into the eyes of the doll and muttered, "I just want to be okay, Mr. Buttoneyes."

The statement caught Sarah unaware and she smiled with hope that they could all be okay again soon. Kate made a wide grin and began to skip beside William and Sarah as they traveled south toward Bogramville.

CHAPTER XXI
AGNITHIA IS CALLED NORTH

Smoke rose out of the holes in the ground and surrounded the peaks of Argenkul. As the sun began to descend toward the horizon in the west a red hue was cast through the haze of death and the long shadows were made harsh in the thick air. The dwarves had ensured that there was no escape from the sheer cliffs where the fortress spires were built. Halls had been carved deep into the foundations of the mountain, but it mattered little as the elves of the Sentinel Woods made sure that they were absolute in their destruction. The general made sure that the army had swiftly overtaken the city gates and purged the surface of dwarves before the enemy army was able to react. Standing atop the peak of the fortress mountain she could feel the souls departing as hall by hall the elven warriors converted the depths of the dwarven stronghold into tombs.

Agnithia Witch-Heart stood facing the setting sun upon the balcony of the mightiest spire near the center of the Argenkul fortress. Her metal mask seemed to shine in the red hue of the sky, the plate blocking all of her natural view, but her gaze seemed wide over the mountain range that swept down into the Midland territory. She reached her hand into the crate that she had carried to the secluded observation and gripped the gnarled orb. As the power within it began to overtake her, and the grain within the wood began to swirl, she uttered, "The dwarves of the peaks have been destroyed, my Queen."

A white light was cast around the balcony as Hissilanda the White held onto the paired gnarl wherever it resided across the lands. "You have done well, Agnithia." The Queen of the Elves appeared before the general as an apparition and seemed to lean over the rail to peer into the haze that surrounded the dwarven fortress.

As the White Queen witnessed the destruction, Agnithia spoke, "So long as the elves in Southrunn continue your efforts, there will be no dwarves south of the Cragged Mountains to concern yourself with any longer."

"I am pleased with your work. Such victories cannot be overlooked. I shall reward you with the spired peaks of Argenkul, as was your desire."

Agnithia bowed her head toward the apparition, "It shall be watched over, my Lady."

"I care not what your intention is with the towers," Hissilanda rejected whatever pleasantries Agnithia was attempting to make. "It would seem that each and every general I have summoned to my command will make some demands of me through this conflict. Even Seedgard made a request for the benefit of his lands, as if it mattered anyway."

Agnithia remained silent as the shining white light of the queen's presence overwhelmed the light of the red sun.

"I am pleased only that your request was in cooperation with my desire. The dwarves of Argenkul are ended. This is good. They will not be able to warn the others or come to aid them now." Hissilanda's image began to dissipate, "Continue toward the eastern side of the dwarven mountains."

"Am I to be called on again?"

"I will need you and your servants to find the way through the paths of Untergak. I believe that is where the dwarves might consider safe, and the paths are too deep to rely on any uncertainty. Your powers to discover those remaining will prove most useful in Helena's Cradle. When you are able you will arrive by my side and we shall continue this campaign to the very end of dwarf kind."

"And of my penance?"

The queen stared at the general while her figure vanished, "We shall see where it is that we all stand when this has ended, Witch-Heart."

The light of the queen vanished and the gnarled wood ceased swirling in Agnithia's hand. With a heavy effort she placed it back into the box beside her and returned her mysterious gaze into the clouds of smoke that signaled their victory to the lands surrounding the mountains.

"General Witch-Heart," The dark moon shaeman was still dressed in the black colors of their homeland, and with an entourage of lesser servants, they appeared at the threshold onto the spire balcony. "We have at last conquered the fortress peaks of Argenkul. No dwarf yet lives in any path of this mountain. The queen has promised it to our dominion if I recall. There will be none left to stop our efforts now."

Agnithia continued to look northward to where the Inland Sea separated the dwarven range from her forest on the northern and western coasts. From her vantage she could witness the great trees of the dark forest heart where her throne still resided. "You were right to warn me when we had gained such a victory in the trade city below." The haze of the carnage from Ovelclutch was still settling in the grasslands to the west. "We have been summoned again. The queen was satisfied with our success. We will need to leave a small garrison here to protect the inner membership. All others who are able have been called by the White Queen to the eastern roads of Helena's Cradle. We will move those of the Twin Rivers north and away from our new dominions."

"Is it still wise to continue the war? We have what it is that we sought. The peaks are ours at last. There is no longer a need to involve ourselves with the concerns of the lesser elvendom."

"Risking the return of dwarves to this place is not the worry that I contend with," Agnithia hissed from beneath the metal mask. "Risking the return of that Queen would be far less wise and far more costly. She is a being of great power. I will follow her for the sake of my own elven dominion, but I would not dare to consider crossing such a thing as her and then allow that power to fester with the thought of our treason."

The darker elf bowed to the general, "I shall prepare those that will be left behind. They will be made ready for their tasks before you leave to continue this matter. The inner members will be awaiting your return."

"I shall meet with the lieutenants and inform them that we will take the passes around the east of the Border Spines. We will not risk inviting the Empire of Man to this war by passing their cities and we must not draw any unwanted attention to these mountains. We must pass through Bilennia's domain, through the Twin River woodlands."

"You would risk venturing into the houses of the elves that still join with Vanessa? The Fey Mother would rebuke you-"

"The White Queen has left us in charge of the forces that answered the calling from that grove land. We will use the noble's invitations and perhaps there are more warriors within those borders that we can induct among our own. Those who have refused to join the effort of the queen will have much more to fear than pretending to cast out the old leaders of Krethnarok into exile."

The dark shaeman nodded and prepared to depart the general, "May darkness hold your secrets."

"You shall be joining me as well," Agnithia demanded. "Ready yourself to continue."

The shaeman was quick to rebuttal, "I am bound to the work of the moon, general. My duty is to complete the tasks of our master. I am not indentured to the White Queen as you."

"Without me your task is doomed." Agnithia turned to face the group at the doorway and the mask seemed to reflect the violent hue of the sky, glowing faintly still despite the waning sunlight. "We are to seek the legendary paths through Untergak, the deepest hole of Nhearn. When we cross through into the sanctuaries of the dwarves there will be none left hiding in any passage. Even you cannot deny how this will benefit our master's efforts. As much as I am needed for your task, I am in need of your servitude. The dark moon assures us of our success."

The dark shaeman grinned with the admittance. "So it shall be."

CHAPTER XXII
BOGRAMVILLE

The moonstone began to flake away in her hands as the low wall of Bogramville came into view. As she thought of her travels the whole way seemed like a blur. They were far to the north in Dwarf Country when she had tasked the enchanted stone with a threshold, but she could not recall if it had been hours, days, or weeks of walking the many spans down the Watcher's Way. Her legs weren't tired and her siblings were not in worse spirits. "Thank you, Reginald," she whispered as the stone became dust in her palm. "Guess I will have to walk all the way back now."

"Where are we," Kate asked.

"This is Bogramville; it's an Imperial port city."

"I don't like the way it feels," William began to complain as they neared the gate. There was a heavy fog around it and the guards who watched the way into the city seemed more grizzled than people they were accustomed to.

"It will be okay, William. Just, both of you, stay close to me."

"It feels loud," William mentioned.

Sarah stopped a moment and listened. There was some noise from the sea, faint shouting of workers and sailors somewhere off in the distance, and the calls of seagulls were infrequent. The route was otherwise silent. "What do you mean?"

"He says it's loud, but that isn't what he means," Kate said as she held tighter to the doll that she had not removed from her grasp since they departed from home.

Sarah's mind tried to wrap around what it could mean and then her heart sank as she realized what was occurring. "Just remember that you have nothing to worry about here, Will." She kneeled down and held his shoulders so that they were focused on each other, "When we get to where we need to be you will not have to worry about anything like this ever again."

"Are we going to stay here long," Kate asked.

"No," Sarah let William go a little so that she could look at Kate as well. "When everything is ready and I have a few sovereigns to spend, we will get on one of the boats here and head north."

"Why north," Kate asked with some confusion.

Sarah was momentarily worried, but the events they found themselves in had also forced Sarah to think quickly and she was sure that even she had forgotten many details through the ordeal. "We have family up in the Northern Territories, up near Meridia."

"Meridia," Kate nodded and it seemed that she was beginning to remember a few trips that their father had taken to visit with the northern DiGardi family.

"That's right. When I am able to get enough money for passage we can leave right from the docks of Bogramville and then we will go to see our family up there." Sarah smiled, hopeful that the idea of future plans would comfort her siblings, even if it was only a little. "We will also get some help for William while we are here. I promise."

Kate and William nodded and Sarah embraced them once more before taking their hands in hers. They approached the guards at the gateway and one of the weathered gate keepers stood up from leaning against the wall. The passage was open, but with a poleaxe the guard halted them, "State your business, mage."

"Heading to the Church of Aurora," she fought through the statement.

"That so?" The guard looked at the other one and made a crooked laugh, "Not many of these Temple folk coming through to see a paladin. Schedule your own funeral, did ya?"

Sarah felt the hands of her siblings clench up with a bit of fright and she tried her best to stay calm for them. "I am sure that *Rapture* wouldn't mind if I atoned a bit."

The guard smiled, "Now that is the first smart thing I've heard from a wizard in all my years, it is." The poleaxe rose up and the guard watched them with an unsavory interest as they entered the city. "Don't make me regret letting one of you in my town now, witch."

The insult would have stung more if she wasn't already trying to hide the truth of their arrival. Sarah entered the fog filled streets of the damp swamp harbor town. It was still midmorning, yet the sunlight couldn't fight through the dark and heavy clouds that seemed so close to raining yet refused to pour. Few citizens were out in the streets, but the ones that were kept their beady eyes fixed on the visitors. She held tightly to the hands of her young brother and sister, darting toward open areas as the sunken foundations of the city structures tilted the dwellings into misshapen narrows and zig-zagging alleyways.

She could see their destination over the mossy rooftops of Bogramville, the steeple point of the church rising up over all else in the city, yet even its obvious presence could not lead her through the maze of poor city planning. She entered into strange streets, passed through oddly shaped plazas, and she encountered one of the more seedy looking taverns twice, though she was sure that this encounter could not have happened without some form of magical interference along their path.

"Are you lost, sister?"

"No, Kate."

"It's ok to say so, if you are."

Sarah was about to spit back, frustrated by needing to bite her tongue while being worried about the foreignness of the town, but she remained composed. Instead she gripped Kate's hand tightly and let it go after a moment. "Sorry, Kate," she had disappointed herself. She took in a deep breath and sighed, "I might be a bit lost. You are right."

"Excuse me," a friendly voice came to them and the grim darkness of the street lifted as the sun found its way through a thinning patch in the fog above the city. "I might be of assistance to you."

Sarah whipped up her red cloak to cover her siblings and she turned in an unfriendly manner toward the assailant. "Who are you?"

"My sincerest apology for any trespass." The stranger raised her hand with two fingers up and then tapped her chest where a holy icon rested by a necklace chain.

"A sister of Christianna," Sarah nodded and relaxed a bit.

"At times," she smiled. The stranger picked up the symbol reverently and displayed it to the red cloaked mage. It was a silver circle with an iron crescent at the top which fitted to the necklace chain. "This is the moon sigil of Aurora and I follow the paths of moonlight, though I am a loyal assistant to the followers of Christianna as well." She placed the holy icon back in its place, "I am the caretaker of the moon shrines along the roads around the swamps so that travelers may find their way and do so with the blessings of the watchful moon."

"You are a daughter of Aurora," Sarah tightened her grip and the brief moment of relaxation was gone.

"Precisely," she bowed politely and kindly smiled at the younger ones. "My name is Magdeline Rissen. When my duties do not call me away from the city I also act as one of the caretakers in the church here in Bogramville."

"Caretaker? You work at the orphanage?"

"I do. The city can be difficult to navigate, especially if you find yourself in unfriendly company. I can lead you on your way if you would like."

Sarah loosened her painful grip on Kate and William. "I could use some help. It would seem I am lost," she shot a frustrated glance at Kate who was smirking with self-awarded victory.

"Do not be so hard on yourself, scholar. You were much closer than you realize." Magdeline took the lead and made only a single turn through an alleyway before they all found themselves in a wide open space where a high mound had been raised. Overlooking the area was a long structure that used every bit of space atop the mound. Magdalene led them to the front of the church beneath the steeple and waited beside the steps up to the doorway. "This is the Church of Moonlight where the Daughters of Moonlight keep vigil. The children can stay here under our care."

"I will be back," Sarah told Magdeline.

"Is the duty of the Mage's Temple going to allow for your return, scholar?"

Sarah could not tell if the Auroran was making a slight at her or was making an honest assessment of her predicament. "Duty to my family will bring me back. We are DiGardi."

"Very noble of you," Magdalene smiled kindly.

"I will be back," Sarah said as she turned to her brother and sister. She fell to her knees and grabbed them both tightly. "Give me a bit of time to make some arrangements. There is a big city not far from here where I can get some sovereigns. We will hire a boat and go north. I will find a home for us again. William, be good and take care of our sister," and she kissed his forehead. "Kate, be strong and stay put. I don't want you getting into any danger," she hugged her tightly. She looked and saw the strange doll in her sister's grip, "Make sure that your brother is cared for too."

"I will," Kate clutched tightly to her sister and the doll.

Sarah let go, stood up quickly, and wiped her eyes from the unexpected wave of tears. "I will be back," she promised. She turned and looked at Magdeline, "I will be back. Whatever is needed I will repay."

The Auroran continued to smile, "We do not keep any accounts of such things. We make sure all children are safe, always. Do not worry, Temple Mage DiGardi," Magdeline lifted her hand again and circled it as the Auroran do for their friends, and then she bowed slightly. "I will keep them safe until then."

"Thank you, moon sister. I am sorry our ways are," she trailed off before saying anything regrettable.

"Need transcends everything."

Sarah found herself smiling at the Auroran and she turned to smile again at each one of her siblings, but she struggled to keep from crying as she turned quickly to leave.

"Wait," Kate's voice halted her. "You didn't say goodbye to Mr. Buttoneyes." Kate held the doll up from under its arms and its limbs swung gently while its sewn mouth rested flat to match the expressionless eyes. It had not once been released by her sister's grip since it was given to her after the fire.

Sarah leaned down and her eyes were on Kate as she said, "Goodbye."

"To Mr. Buttoneyes," Kate shook the doll to fix Sarah's attention onto it.

"Goodbye, Mr. Buttoneyes," Sarah stared into the horrific doll's eyes and for a moment the black glass buttons appeared differently than before. Her gaze met her sister again as the doll returned to Kate's embrace. Kate and Mr. Buttoneyes seemed at last satisfied with the farewell. "I will be back," she said one last time to them before leaving the church yard with haste.

CHAPTER XXIII
HISSILANDA THROUGH THE PLAINS

The plain elves went to each of the queen's lieutenants as the first showings of dawn began on the eastern horizon. Carts that had been pulled along by stag were halted so that the encampment supplies could be hauled out and the soldiers went to work building scaffolding that the plainer nomads had supplied along with colorful textiles to craft shade before the morning sun arrived.

The elven armies had been moving through the endless grasslands of the Great Plains slower than they had anticipated, their marches occurring only as the plainer elves directed and only throughout the nights. Many of the queen's lieutenants were vocal about the need to march continuously to keep the element of surprise before the dwarven holds received word that there had been an attack, but the White Queen herself demanded that all of the elven forces follow the recommendations of the nomads who knew the dangers of traveling across the open lands.

"Chieftain Selo'Hema," the queen respectfully called to the plainer elf that had refused the title of general from her offering. "Where are we now across your lands? We move only at night at your request and we are not familiar enough with your landmarks to guess our whereabouts."

He hid his eyes as he looked upon the radiant light of Hissilanda in the dark. "My queen, the open sun would ruin our rations and exhaust your warriors before we make it across the grass."

"You are the master of this land. I apologize on behalf of the lieutenants under my command. They assume that their holy homeland gives them more experience abroad than they are deserved. Many of them have never left the shade of Krethnarok's canopy in their lifetime."

"They are arrogant because I have led them right and they do not know of the struggle they would have endured otherwise. It is the same with our youngers who act before they know the wisdom of their forebears." Chief Selo'Hema pointed toward the dark sky northward and westward. "Your answer, my queen, the sun will reveal where we have come."

The elven army had only been moving at night since the departure from Ovelclutch, and at each morning the wood elves among the force would grumble that no landmarks could be seen, not even the high peak of Aboraeve. The wood elves were also upset with the endlessness of the Great Plains, that days of marching had yielded no noticeable ground. As the elves finished making camp before dawn once more, setting up the scaffoldings and stretching the canvas for the shade through the day, the silhouettes of the mountains began to reveal themselves, and a murmur among the elven host began to make guesses as to what slopes stood before them.

Where Chief Selo'Hema pointed, shown by the rising sun in the east, was the gap of the Imitheon Valley. Hissilanda looked to the north and could see the sheer cliffs of the Cragged Mountains making sharp shadows in the rays of the low morning sun. There was a ridge that came southward and it appeared to enter into the plains just a bit east from where they were setting camp for the day. She knew that the Empire of Man had a fortress at the foot of that arm from the mountains and she smirked as their position favored avoiding interaction with the humans.

South of the wide chasm of the Imitheon Valley were the sharp sudden rises of the Black Mountain Range however. As Hissilanda scanned the landscape for signs of any obstacles before them, the plainer elves began to whisper, all of them facing the dark mountains appearing in the morning light. They were reciting a poem, or perhaps a prayer, or it could have been an oath, but they all recited the same words together as they saw the dark volcanic rock that ended their dominion abruptly along the eastern border of the Great Plains.

"E're do om e'aht ganna thorbranni.
E'n e're el mun ec thorbranni.
E're do el ne're sha thorbranni.
E'n e're el fol ec thorbranni
O're ec thorbranni"

"Chief Selo'Hema," Hissilanda waited for him to end his words to get his fixed attention. "What is this that you have all uttered?"

"It is a pledge from the *Elder Days*, from the time of our forebears, from long before the Great War, even before a time when Aelum'Hau was revered."

"You speak of the Age of Woe," Hissilanda answered.

"From the ancient days we have kept that mountain range in our thoughts. It is the last defense before the end."

Hissilanda looked at the sharp dark rock with the chief. "It is the wall of the orc, you mean."

"No, it is the wall for us. That is the prison of Montontra," the chief stared at the ridge of mountains with a deep anger. "It is where the fire lives, where the light begins and the glow lingers. It is where the doom of the world will begin, where the fall of life is brewing."

"Morganna of Fire," Hissilanda knew of what threat the plain elves worried for.

"In time the prison of the earth will not be able to hold her, and the border of the sea will only direct the path into this land, and it will be that our people will stand against it." Chief Selo'Hema took a deep breath as he turned to the queen, standing tall before her with a proud burden. "We will be where the fire begins. We will stand as the moon stands against the evils. We will be blessed by the air and by the fey in their graces. We will be blessed by even the light of Heaven. We will be there when the end comes, and we will triumph over the fire at last."

"What do you expect of me," Hissilanda questioned coldly.

"If Katrina has not given you her song, I expect you to do as you will."

Hissilanda had waited for the leader of the plainer elves to make a request of her as the other generals had, and she was pleasantly surprised when such a request did not come from the plainer elf. She turned and looked once more at the tall stone border of the Cragged Mountains which stood between them and the mountain passages of Helena's Cradle. Her white glow seemed less intense than it had beneath the stars and she put a hand on the shoulder of the plainer elf. "Forgive me when my triumph comes, for I would not wish harm to my kin among the grasses."

Chief Selo'Hema thought for a moment at what she had meant by that, and then he bowed as the queen left to strategize further with the other elves of leadership.

CHAPTER XXIV
THE HUNTERS ARRIVE

The sky was becoming a deeper shade of gray as night descended over the coast. The two sisters could begin to see the twinkling lamps of Bogramville coming to life, but what struck their senses first was the smell of the fishing wharf which was still foul from baking in the sun through the evening. Their silver eyes scanned across the rooftops over the wall of the decently sized city. It was a good deal larger than other Imperial places they had encountered across the Midlands, though it was not as populated as the nearby throne city of Tronia, nor was it as well defended as the southern city of Shilo, but from where they walked on the raised levee road they could see the masts of large trade ships docked at the bustling port of the Imperial city.

Evelyn's eyes darted about and she caught the tall silhouette of the large gray Legion fortress whose barracks could potentially manage a military garrison numbering in the hundreds. "We will be gone before they need to be aware," Alison noticed the focus in her sister's eyes. "We will not need to involve them this time."

"I am sorry once again, sister. I was unaware that the witch was on active duty at the time."

They both neared the city gate at the tip of the northern peninsula of the Crab Bay, finishing their long journey around the levee structure of the Swamp of Zemeg. As they came to the threshold of Bogramville, heavy clouds of mist gathered from the marshes in the darkness to envelope the city for the night and soak a terrible damp into the foundations of the dwellings.

Alison approached the gate first as her sister fell a few paces behind in her study of the city. The entrance was little more than piled stone mortared together so that it stood only two heights tall, and in most of the grooves between the stones were heavy patches of moss that were as dark green as the swamp kelps. A lone guard with a torch-pole stood at the gateway, a horn to his waist, and not much more than a cudgel to defend himself. "Hail there," he lifted the pole to get the light on the coming guest. The silver moon symbol reflected from her breastplate in the torchlight, but it was her silver eyes that glowed bright in the coming dark that offered her true identity. "An Auroran? Welcome, paladin. I hope you've come to aid us folk 'ere. In desperate need we are."

Alison's voice was still and emotionless as she acknowledged the Imperial watchman. "I intend to help, but the violence will be daunting."

"We don't want violence, miss," he said with a fair bit of shock. "We don't 'ave big problems for all that now. These docks 'ere are peaceful 'nough."

"They are plagued," she corrected the guard. "So much so that there is strife. Struggle dwells here," she kept still, but her silver lit eyes moved about as she studied the city through the open arched gateway. "That is how evil takes root. I hope to save you from as much of it as I am able."

The guard took an uneasy step out of her way. "Far be it from me to in'erfere with the work of an Auroran."

Alison walked passed him and shortly behind her arrived Evelyn whose silver eyes were more fearsome with the passing of time into darker night. She did not blink as she neared the gate watcher. "Auroran business, let me pass."

"Two of ya?" The watchman took another step away from the gate to let the paladin pass him. "Christianna protect and bless us this night."

Evelyn suddenly stopped as she was passing and it frightened the guard. She slowly turned her head to stare into his eyes and even the flames of his torch seemed to halt before the Auroran's fearsome presence. "Christianna? We call her *'The One Who Watches'*," and then she continued through the open gate with an audible scoff.

Inside the wall of stone the buildings were saturated and the wood beams were swollen with dampness. The shingles were disgruntled and in every nook there grew thick green moss in heavy wet clumps. Lamps were lit at street corners, but the light was weak and the city was kept in a misty dark. Both of their silver eyes darted about at the subtle movements in the night and caught the nocturnal denizens wandering in the alley ways.

"Something is keeping them awake," Evelyn muttered.

"There is something that makes it hard for them to find their homes," Alison added. "It is the sickness that was invited here."

"Witches," Evelyn smirked. She changed her posture so that the dark blade on her back touched her more closely. It was vibrating with the anticipation of a new hunt. Her eyes fell upon the hilt of her sister's sword and the green gemstone fixed within the cross guard was glowing in a sickly pale hue as it consumed the Winds of Magic from the air around them. "This place is permeated with wild magics."

"It is no wonder that Calcifor gave this errand to us before we are to set off on our own."

They both moved through the city quickly, passing through plazas and off-centered alleyways, but their pathway was made clear as they followed the humming of their blades to the source of the untamed magic. As they rounded the corner out of one of the many oddly shaped plazas, they approached the rise overlooking the water upon which a large building with a steep roof had been built, the nooks and crannies just as unkempt and grown with moss as any other dwelling in Bogramville. At the top of its high steeple was the double iron cross of Christianna, the sign of the church.

They crossed the grounds with purpose and came to the head of the mound where the entryway into the church awaited them. There were four sharp steps leading to the door and above the swollen wood entry was another double iron cross marking the threshold of Christianna's home. Above the holy symbol, which was an incredibly uncommon presentation in shared shrine spaces, was a silvered disk, symbol of the moon and of Aurora. Evelyn spat at the first step. "It is a wasted den. Sad to see our homes offered to the utility of our enemies."

Alison's eyes scanned the area to see any movements within. In the dark, the shadows near the sconce light against the church windows were easy to catch. The front door opened with gentle care and holding a grease lantern was an armored brother of the order, a paladin warrior of Aurora. He held the lantern high, but he could see them both plainly, their silver eyes glowing in the night, both sets of eyes fixated upon him. "Welcome, moon sisters."

Alison took the steps up to the doorway and forced the paladin aside with surprising strength. "I wish we had come to be welcomed. Aurora has seen the efforts of the Church of Moonlight." She opened the door without the same care as the other Auroran had done and then entered into the main hall of the church.

As the paladin turned to ask further questions, Evelyn swiftly rose the stairs and her blade cared little against the thick armor that he bore. As he slumped away, she took hold of his lamp, and the body clattered down each stair until it clanged against the ground.

Startled by the noise outside, the Christiannan priest within the hall turned to face the guest who he had assumed was the paladin returning inside. "Oh. Welcome, daughter of Aurora," the clergyman bowed. He had a long match and only half of the shrine's candles were yet lit.

Alison slowly moved across the creaking floorboards of the church hall toward the priest. "I must offer apologies to Christianna, for her house is a necessary casualty in my duties."

The priest squinted at her through his bushy brow, "Beg my pardon, Auroran. I do not understand."

Inside of the large room, gathered along the walls, were table shrines to various saints, and at the rear of the room was a stage raised by a single step on which a pedestal sat with a holy book of prayer, closed, but bookmarked with a golden ribbon where the priest may have been studying. Behind this stage, positioned on either side, was a pair of doors leading to the living quarters, and above those doors were the protective vigils of the full moon represented by silvered disks.

After observing the area her gaze fell back onto the priest. "You have been harboring the blighted behind the protection of the Lady of the Moon?"

"Yes," the priest answered in a tremble. "Why must they," but his words trailed into a hushed mumble as a powerful glow consumed the windows flanking the front door.

"Utmost, evil must be ended," Alison said to answer all of the questions he may have remaining.

Nearly the whole worship hall was alight and the front door was fully engulfed in inescapable flame. Alison was quick to release the clergyman, his sinless ways allowing for her to gift him swift mercy from the coming torrent, and she moved to the rear quarters. Without hesitation she opened the way, sure that the vigil of Aurora would not betray her through the necessary duty she had been tasked with.

Her eyes quickly took in the scene before her. About the large chamber were partitions to cut the space into equal rooms. Each room appeared to be equipped with bunks that were each three beds high, most every bed housing a restless child still asleep despite the coming horror. In the quarters were also daughters of the moon, Aurorans who cared for the shrines and offered themselves to the Goddess in alternative ways to fighting. Most were asleep, but a few meandered through the area completing their routines for the night.

A heavy thud as the door closed caught the attention of one member and their head jerked toward Alison who had arrived. "The way is shut," she stated. "Aurora calls. Your sinful ways shall be ended and justice shall be done." The floor boards creaked as the shrine tender struck the floor. The others then took notice and fled through a door at the far end of the chamber.

Alison was not afraid to do what was necessary, though Aurora herself would have wished there was another way. The roar of fire had consumed the church already and the door into the quarters was hissing as the damp of Bogramville began to leave it. At every bunk was a thick wooden door and each threshold was fashioned with a metal bar inscribed with dwarven runes. *Magic wards,* she thought to herself. *They know what they have been doing.*

She closed the first bedroom door and set the bar into place so that it could not be opened from within. She could feel the humming of her blade dampen slightly as the dwarven runes hid the magic inside the rooms. The way was shut and the witch within had been subdued. She then did the same for the next door, and so on, until all the bunks were sealed so that the illness was trapped. At the last door, Alison set to close the way and place the bar, but her silver eyes peeked within and caught sight of a little girl sitting upright who was staring back at her.

"Hello," the girl said kindly from the humble bunk.

"I see you, child. Hello," Alison answered, trying to pierce the girl with her moon lit sight.

"Why are you here, master paladin?"

Honesty was Alison's way, always. "I am cleansing the church of sin." Her silver eyes glowed, but the light could not shine through the girl. Alison's blade made no mention of magic, the usual humming near witches was quelled by the dwarven runes around the orphanage, but the black sword hushed more so as it neared the girl. "Why are you here, child?"

"My sister brought me. She needed time to get some sovereigns. She studies at the Temple, so she had no place else to take us after the accident. She'll be back soon and then we are going to Meridia up north."

Alison rarely felt hesitation, but this child was eluding her, potentially overpowering her. *Unlikely*, she comforted her mind. "Child," Alison outstretched her hand to invite the girl to leave. "Come with me now."

"I was asked to stay here, to be safe."

"I will guarantee that you will be safer than if you were to remain here. This place is the den of sin."

The girl looked around the small room and then looked into the eyes of a doll that she had been gripping too tightly. She whispered a bit to the doll and nodded as it made some quiet pretend reply to her. "I am supposed to be going north with my sister. Will you take me there, master paladin?"

"My road may lead that way. I have not yet been bound to a new direction. Come," Alison demanded.

Shyly, the girl stood up and went to take Alison's hand, her arm still bound tightly about the doll. "Will I be able to see my brother?"

"It may yet be too late. The time of pleasantness in this church is over and those within are now in the fates of Aurora."

The girl nodded, she did not cry or argue, but clutched to the huntress, and they wandered out of the rear door where Evelyn closed the way with an eager speed. Evelyn moved to wait below the rise of the church, stepping over the severed bodies of those who had attempted to escape their fate, and stared at the girl as Alison led the child by the hand away from the destruction. She said nothing, assuming her sister had reason for such an unusual intervention.

The three of them departed from Bogramville as the flames of the church began to raise the alarms of the city. Bells from the Legion fortress rang as they passed through the arch of the city gate. Screams and panicked attempts to squelch the fire came on the wind to terrorize them as they took the road eastward, but none of them, not even the young girl who had been taken away, could be haunted by the noise as it grew fainter with distance.

CHAPTER XXV
THE BLACKROOT
CROSS THE PLAINS

The grasslands were vast and Agnithia's warning of needing a guide had proven true. They had a good heading and made good time, but the endless grasses in all directions had led them astray a few times during their passage. At last they could see ahead of them the impassible sharp dark rock of the eastern edge of the Black Range Mountains. They continued directly to the end of the Great Plains and Terica let out a sigh of relief, "There is a road. At least there is something to follow."

"This must be the Watcher's Way," Lilium scanned the roadway for anything passing through the hills at the edge of the mountains. "That would mean that we are a bit south of where we were meant to go."

"I am rested enough for it. We can still make up the time." Terica looked at the older assassin who was in deep and despairing thoughts. "The Imperial roads are not too bad. After that brief bit on the Marching Road I can appreciate what the humans are trying to do. I might even try to thank the Empire of Man for it someday."

As Lilium finally shifted her gaze toward her companion, she fixed her expression into a smile and said, "That is an optimistic view of our predicament."

"Have you thought of what you are meant to do?"

Lilium had a moment of excitement then, her eyes lit up as though she knew the answer to the question that had been gnawing at her, but then her expression drifted back into concern that she would never truly know it. "Let me think about it a bit longer." She reached down and made sure that the vile blade was still in its simple wrappings at her side. As her fingers touched the weapon, her companion could see that the evil was wrapping itself around Lilium, clouding her mind and punishing her for holding onto it. "This thing can only work one time. I must be absolutely sure."

"Are the dreams helping? I have not had them as badly these last few nights."

"They are, and they offer me more than you know."

"Conversation, you mean? To get your mind off of what you carry there?"

"Well," Lilium lowered her eyes toward the dagger before she returned to see her companion smiling back at her. For a moment she did feel distance between her and the evil blade. The dim that had been surrounding her seemed to brighten and she began to notice the sun shining on her skin. "Yes, it has been a welcomed distraction."

They set foot onto the road and followed the path northward, rising up and over the grassy hills, though they avoided Imperial villages that had been built along the way, each of the settlements taking up space on the other side of the road to avoid upsetting the elven lands east of the Watcher's Way. There were enough farmlands among the villages to sustain trade, which Lilium and Terica were able to see the carriages and carts long before they were able to see them, and they avoided the wanderers with ease. The road, comfortable, free of debris, and hosting a clear direction, proved invaluable for making up any lost time the assassin's had spent in crossing through the Great Plains.

The Cragged Mountains made their appearance, and after some more long days of walking the Watcher's Way, the two arrived at the opening of the Imitheon Valley. The Black Range cornered harshly, the black jagged rock still guarding entry into the lands within, and at the only passage into Montontra was a fortress belonging to the Empire of Man to keep guard from the orc. Terica looked toward the Cragged Mountain side of the valley and discovered the view of the Snake Road. It carved up the sheer cliff face so that the roads formed a diamond pattern all the way to the top of a mountain ravine near a plateau in the high slopes. Lilium studied the two ridges of the Cragged Mountains that further enclosed the way ahead, one reaching toward the south into the Great Plains while the other sloped out of sight into the west toward what she assumed was Dwarf Country.

"The way is quiet," Lilium's eyes became sharp as she scanned the flat land between all of the mountain ranges. "The pass ahead is narrow as well."

"There must be plenty wandering through here that we would go unnoticed," Terica offered.

"Very few." Lilium could make out a few distant figures that were crossing through the Imitheon Valley. "But the fortress there, the Watcher's Keep, if I know it from story, it does not keep eyes on the valley floor."

"What does it watch then?"

"Orc. Fire orc, from Morganna's lands."

Terica looked at the slopes again, gazing over the landscape for strategic elements, and at the tip of the southern arm from the Cragged Mountains was a wall that protected the road. "That fortress is the one that keeps its eyes on the valley."

"There is likely to be another at the other tip of the mountains then. The Empire of Man is thorough in keeping its borders defended. So far they have been pleasant enough to keep to their agreements with the plain elves."

"No one will bother with two travelers, and the humans would deal with us less if they knew that we were elves, I would assume," Terica thought of the next leg of the journey aloud. "But the roads here are so trampled by the Imperial soldiers, I cannot tell if the elves have already passed or not."

"Then we must risk it either way." Lilium started walking along the Watcher's Way into the Imitheon Valley, though quickly their path faded into the many other roads that crisscrossed over the flat land. The signs around them were many, though none of them seemed to rest beside a particular roadway, and they all only pointed to destinations of interest around the valley, avoiding matching their purpose to anything that appeared in the likeness of a path.

They wandered without being accosted by other travelers or tradesmen across the flat land. As they continued they found that all of the trodden or rutted treks through the valley began to tighten and intertwine themselves into a single road out of the quiet shadows of the mountains. They kept the Black Mountain Range to their south to follow the dark rock out into the west,

and after many distances they began to see the bank of
fog that sat over the western coast.

CHAPTER XXVI
BASIMICK'S CHOICE

The writ and token had proven useful for the time he had spent in the city. The inn had been pleasant enough and provisions from the innkeeper's personal stores were offered with great enthusiasm. He had thought to deny such gracious care, but the Empire would pay any debt and the king of Imitheon was responsible for financing the hunter's lengthy business.

After wallowing in his sorrow, Basimick left his rented room, carried himself down the stairs to the inn's first floor tavern, crossed the busy space, and left quietly through the front door. Basimick then entered the misty streets where people wandered in and out of view like shadows. There were crowds in plenty, soldiers marching, and business within the many storefronts seemed good at this hour, but the mountain mist of Imitheon kept them all to a whisper.

As he made his way to the lower terraces of the city, he became more aware that the crowds were hushing themselves when he neared so that they could watch as a dragon hunter passed them by. He began moving quicker as shame began to overtake him. Perhaps they didn't see a hunter at all, just a refugee with a coat he didn't earn.

Basimick lowered his head and continued to the gate at the bottom tiers of the city with haste to avoid any more exposure with the citizens of an Empire he had sworn to protect.

He was dizzy as the soldiers keeping watch over the gate let him out of Imitheon, his thoughts ceaselessly racing with questions and quandaries that further darkened his mood. He tried to answer them as best he could, speaking back against himself as the thoughts appeared to him without a moment of peace. *I had no choice. I am a hunter of the Empire. I was forced into something I did not know anything about. I must run away and hide. I must confront the dragon or lose my honor. It is my duty to serve the people. I continue to serve because of my shame. My father would be disappointed with what I have done. I have killed my family and I have destroyed my home. I was doing what I thought was right. I should have listened to him. I should have listened.*

It was humiliating and his mind became fixated on his failure. His legs took him away from the city. Without noticing he crossed the farmlands to the edge of the Imitheon Plateau and he went all the way down the switch backing turns of the Snake Road in despair. The way led out of the shadow of the cliff side and met the Trade Road. He stood in the middle of a rutted crossway which was vacant of travelers for as far as he could see through the Imitheon Valley. The intersection kept him in place and, though the thoughts did not stop coming to him, he took a moment to think of what he had to do next.

He looked east and was reminded of home, but the thought of returning to the quiet scorch mark that had once been the village of Kurrum with so little accomplished haunted his heart. He peered south where he could see the dark clouds in the land of fire beyond the Black Mountain Range, into the lands of Montontra. He had injured the dragon once and it was easy for his mind to imagine a victory if he could just find its lair. Basimick turned to gaze west where one of the many signs littered about the roadways pointed toward Presons and the further dwarven regions. He knew that was where the elves would be heading, if they had not passed through the Imitheon Valley already, and if he were in time, perhaps he could change the fate of that place.

The valley between the outstretched arms of the Cragged Mountains and the north face of the Black Range was terribly quiet. He looked again toward the south and the narrow passage through the Mouth of Montontra appeared to open wider before him. There was a gap in the peaks of jagged black stone where he could simply walk into Montontra itself, though he had been well warned by many throughout his life regarding the terrible orc that lived in that foul place. They were the minions of a great power that dwelt in the fires of that land and such a wicked divinity could drive them to powerful violence easily. Beside the entry to the crevice in the mountain range was an Imperial fortress, a tower that could peer into the passage, and the stories of danger became more real at the sight of it. His gaze followed the wall of the Watcher's Keep and returned into the depths of the vile place. It was clear for the moment and even at this distance he could see the great volcano's explosive glare on the black smoke clouds in the deeper distances within the Mouth of Montontra. Wherever that mountain was is where Olag of Fire was sure to be.

He took several steps toward that evil land, and then he hesitated to look west. Across the flat scape of the Imitheon Valley, out into the lands toward the western coast, where beyond the view of the Cragged Mountains and the saw tooth peaks of the Black Mountain Range, sat the city of Presons.

Basimick was torn, both ways set before him and only his own choice to guide him. He thought about Ulric who spoke at length of his thoughts on matters of the Empire and of gray morals when he had been choosing his own paths in life. He could recall Terica, during the comforts of the mud pits, who had shared some of the elven plans with him for hope that he could help aid in a greater purpose. He dwelled on Cassius and Longinus who had put such faith in him that they sacrificed themselves so that he could save more lives than any hunter ever had before them. Above all these memories he encountered though, he dwelled on the thoughts of his family most.

"Where do I go, master Bassar," he said aloud, half joking but whole heartedly hoping an answer would arrive. The roads now seemed eager for an answer as the ruts across the ground became more and more noticeable, stretching deep into the golden grassy fields, into the mountains all around him, toward the green hills beyond the valley, out to each horizon, and he fell into deeper thought about what he was *meant* to do.

The way west to Presons now reminded him of Ovelclutch, the war, death indiscriminate, and the hate of the elves so vast that it was beyond all the emotion he could dare to comprehend. He shifted and looked south at Montontra. He pulled the coin out of his pocket and turned his hunter's token over in his hand before taking out the other two. He looked at them to remember Cassius and Longinus who hunted tirelessly for the beast, doing so selflessly for the good of all

Nhearn. He thought of his family, of Kurrum, and especially he dwelt on his father.

"I suppose Presons can handle itself." He readjusted the traveling pack over his shoulder and set his heading south. Basimick managed only a few steps when he was stricken with sudden gloom. "It's not on me to save everyone." As he said it, Basimick realized he was only pretending to be a selfless dragon hunter. "Revenge is as fine a motivation as any," he admitted to nobody but himself.

Basimick tried again to walk south when another wave of guilt halted him. It felt as though a powerful person was pushing into his chest and breathing became difficult for him. He forced another step forward, hoping that overcoming this barrier might give him the confidence to speak with the dragon Olag during their next meeting. Another step south and suddenly above him was the cawing of a lone bird.

The valley had been quiet and from nowhere a black crow had appeared overhead, breaking the silence while it circled ever lower toward Basimick. He watched as the bird fell lower and lower until at last it landed beside him at the corner of the south path to Montontra and the west road to Presons.

"You must be the sign I was asking for then," Basimick spoke to the bird and noticed now it was of a large stature. It did not entertain him by cawing, nor did it fly away to be forgotten, it simply sat before him as though it too wanted a choice to be made. "The dragon is as dangerous as any army. Slaying it will be honorable," but the bird did not answer him back. Basimick looked at the volcanic haze in the passage once again. "But leaving so many to die," he felt the duty of Kurrum swell in his chest. He was an acting captain of the watch of an Imperial hold as much as he was a dragon hunter, if both titles could be held onto at once.

"What is my duty," Basimick asked the crow, hoping that in some way the bird could offer him an answer.

The crow then made a loud commotion and its wings beat fiercely as it lifted itself up off the ground and circled once again over the crossroad. Basimick stared at the crow and looked at the passage into the deadly lands of the orc. He was not afraid of what was ahead, but the bravado became recognizable as he began to calm his nerves. *Neither a bow nor a companion to fight a dragon,* he thought to himself.

He looked up at the circling crow and asked, "Do good people know how to make good choices?"

He nodded, knowing that his answer felt like the right decision. As he stepped on the road to the western city of Presons he found that his legs were not hindered, nor his breathing overtaken by some strong entity, but that his heart was emboldened by what he knew was right. He would need to save who he could. It was a duty that was beyond that of a watchman, or even that of a dragon hunter. It was a purpose that good folk must choose to do. The crow then made a loud caw to signal Basimick's passing westward before it lifted away into the sky in a gentle breeze. With ease Basimick passed the signpost that pointed the way and he began his journey west along the Trade Road toward Presons.

Iron Gate
Dwamaklad
Dwarf Country
THE GREAT BAY
Pessonian Woods
Presons
Trade Road
Delceon
HELENA'S CR
Stoneway
Imitheon M
Snake Road
Watcher's Keep
The Mouth
Felceon
Cragg
Mhat-Ozogra
Grasstown
MONTONTRA
THE DREAD STRAIGHT
Black Range
Watcher's Way
THE
LUSH
LANDS
Green Watch
Troni
WEST-GATE SEA
Swamps of Zemeg
Nemegan
Bogramville

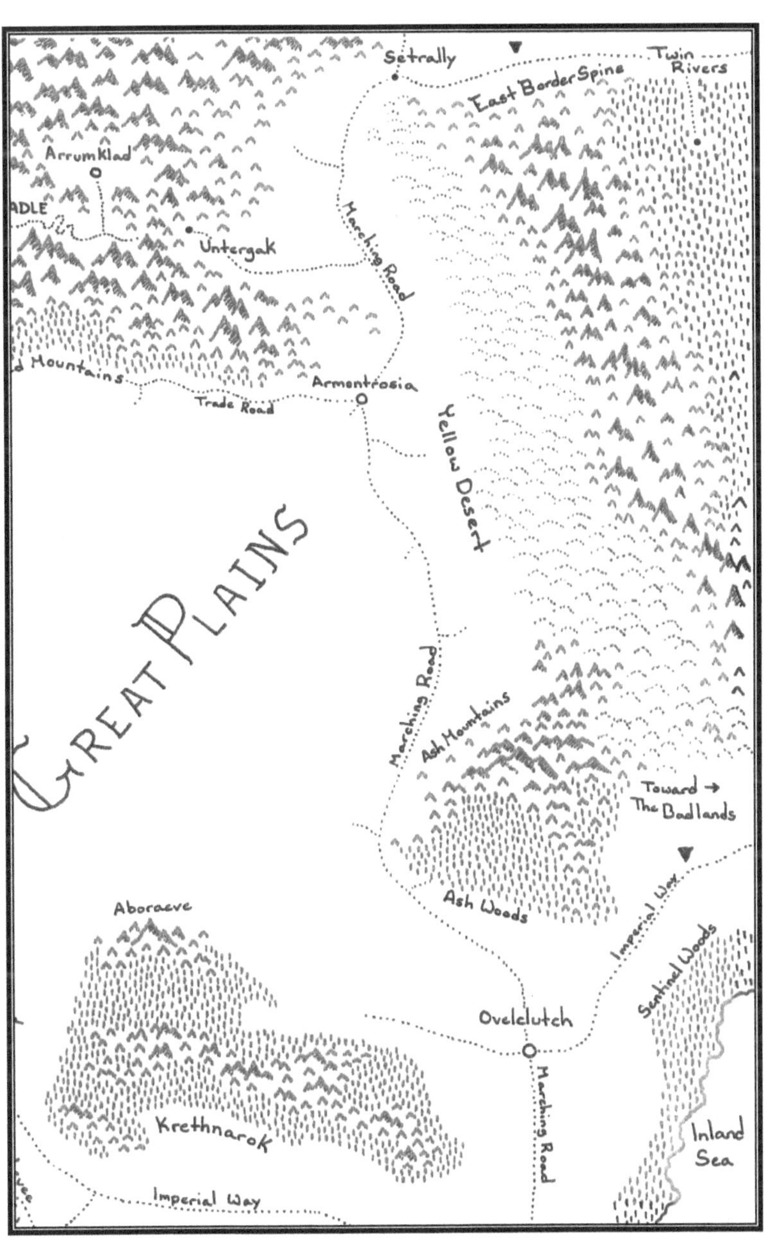

Setrally
Twin Rivers
East Border Spine
ArrumKlad
ADLE
Untergak
Marching Road
d Mountains
Trade Road
Armentrosia
Yellow Desert
GREAT PLAINS
Marching Road
Ash Mountains
Toward →
The Badlands
Imperial Way
Ash Woods
Aboraeve
Sentinel Woods
Ovelclutch
Krethnarok
Marching Road
Inland Sea
ee
Imperial Way